OFF LIMITS: THE CELEBRITY

KAT BELLEMORE

KB PRESS

ALSO BY KAT BELLEMORE

OFF LIMITS: YA Romantic Comedy

Off Limits: The Best Friend

Off Limits: The Smarty Pants

Off Limits: The Scrooge

Off Limits: The Principal's Son

Off Limits: The Celebrity

BORROWING AMOR: Small Town Romance

Borrowing Amor

Borrowing Love

Borrowing a Fiancé

Borrowing a Billionaire

Borrowing Kisses

Borrowing Second Chances

STARLIGHT RIDGE: Beach Romance

Diving into Love

Resisting Love

Starlight Love

Building On Love

Winning his Love

1

SCOTT

Scott stumbled into bed, not completely sure what time it was, but the light slipping past his curtains was not a good sign. It meant that his parents would be in shortly to harass him about going to school. It was funny how they still thought that kind of thing mattered. Hadn't they figured out yet that details of the War of 1812 or Pythagoras's theorem weren't going to get him a job?

Besides, Scott already had one of those, and it paid him a whole heck of a lot more than anything else he'd ever go after. Even more than his parents' jobs. Combined. A lot more.

Knock-knock.

At least they still bothered to announce their presence. As if they cared about his privacy. As if they didn't try to control every aspect of his life.

Scott didn't answer, instead closing his eyes and slowing his breathing. Better to pretend to be asleep. He was so tired, in another minute he wouldn't have to fake it.

But he heard the knob twisting. The door opening. The soft footsteps of his mother. At least it was her. Now there was a chance of him staying home.

The bed sank on one edge as his mom sat, her hand resting lightly on his arm. She smelled like her favorite cucumber lotion.

"Hey, Scotty, rise and shine."

He groaned in response, like she'd just woken him.

"Nice try, but no getting out of it today. Not if you're going to graduate."

Scott opened his eyes and flopped over so he could see his mom. She was dressed in her usual pantsuit, ready to go to the law office. Scott had told her she didn't need to work as a legal assistant anymore—a job she hated. He'd take care of her. But she refused to quit.

"What's the point, Mom? I already know everything there is to making it in life, and I didn't need a piece of paper to do it. Besides, I have my private tutor when I'm on the road. That counts toward graduation, right?"

Her lips pursed. They'd had this conversation many times, and neither had managed to sway the other to their point of view.

"If you'd actually listened to him and done the work, yes, it would have." She paused. "I know you love music. And you're crazy talented, and the world had the sense to notice it. But nothing can replace a good education. The entertainment industry is a fickle business, and there's no guarantee that in five years you'll still be playing sold-out stadiums."

Yes, they'd had that conversation too.

"Then why did Matt's parents give him full control of his career, including his finances? Jordan has full control too."

His mom released a long sigh and rubbed the bridge of her nose. "Which is why you were out all night. Bungee jumping off Jordan's roof. Three stories up. While his parents are out of town for their anniversary."

So, she knew. That was fast, even for her.

"You could have been hurt," she said, and Scott subconsciously touched one of the many bruises he'd gotten over the course of the evening. "Your friends... I know their parents are doing the best they can. This is uncharted territory for all of us. But Matt and Jordan spend their money as quickly as they make it, which is a feat with how well your band has been doing."

Annoyance bubbled in Scott's chest. "You make it sound like we're still fourteen and playing in the garage."

"I sometimes wish that were true," his mom said, her voice sad. "You boys had so much fun. I never had to worry about where you were, because you were either playing your hearts out in our garage or you were in the kitchen, eating everything you could get your hands on." She paused. "Now? I pray every night that you'll come home safe."

Guilt pricked at Scott, but he pushed it away. He wasn't a little boy anymore. He was seventeen, and he had made more money in the last three years than his parents had in the last twenty. Scott had also traveled further than either of them—had more experiences. Who were they to lecture him on finances or life choices? The problem was that they didn't trust him. They never gave him a chance to prove himself, instead insisting that they knew best.

Once he turned eighteen, all that was going to change.

"I'm not going to school," Scott said, then turned his back to his mom. He had some sleep to catch up on.

His mom didn't leave. "You can't hang in there for three more months? You're so close."

Three more months to the end of the school year, but only seventy-two days until his birthday. Not that he was counting.

Scott heard a sniffle and turned back to his mom. Her eyes were moist, a few stray tears making trails down her cheeks. He sat up all the way and pulled her into a hug.

"I'm sorry, Mom," he murmured. "I just... I can't do it

anymore. Not even for three months. You don't know what it's like to go to that school every day. If I still had Jordan and Matt, it might be different. But once they left..."

His mom surprised him by pulling away and standing. "They don't go to school either?" She gave a small shake of her head. "This wasn't the life I wanted for you. Or them. You were good kids."

Before Scott could answer, she left, shutting the door behind her.

He had won that battle. No school for him today. So why did it feel like a loss? Scott snuggled back under his down comforter, but he couldn't sleep, his mind now too busy, his mom's words playing on repeat. Sure, he partied a bit and skipped school when he was tired and not wanting to deal with people. Which was nearly every day.

But he was still a good guy—wasn't he?

SOMETHING WAS OFF.

A thick tension had settled over the house the past couple of weeks, and as Scott shoved his phone into his pocket, a sense of foreboding accompanied it. Hopefully he could slip downstairs unnoticed. He'd been avoiding his parents whenever possible, and they seemed to be returning the favor. His mom didn't even bother getting him up for school anymore.

Scott walked down the two flights of stairs from his room at the very top of the house. Most would say he lived in the attic, but he preferred "private quarters." His parents sat in the front room, papers spread around them. Scott's foot squeaked against the wood as he moved off the last step, and both their gazes swung toward him. His mom looked guilty.

Whatever this was, it wasn't good.

"Going out," he said. "Don't wait up."

Scott knew his mom would stay up anyway. She couldn't sleep whenever he was out late, no matter how many times he told her not to worry—that her staying up all night didn't help either of them.

"Just a minute, Scott," his dad said, straightening. "We have a couple of things to talk about before you go out with your friends." When Scott opened his mouth to protest, his dad interrupted before he had the chance. "It's important. And it needs to happen. Now."

Scott's dad was a manager of a local bank, and he knew how to deliver bad news. He had that same aura about him now, his gaze piercing.

Scott knew better than to argue with that look. He moved into the room and sat on the couch across from his parents. He hated that couch. It was eighteen years old—a gift to his mom when she was pregnant with him. His mom said it held memories, but Scott thought it probably held more dirt and dust than anything. He wished his parents would let him buy them a new couch. A new house. All the things they deserved but would never accept. Not from their seventeen-year-old son.

"You're throwing away your future," his dad started in, skipping any niceties. Scott supposed they were past those at this point.

"If you hadn't noticed, I'm doing pretty well. New album. Going out on my third tour at the end of the summer. People can't get enough of me."

"But that won't last forever," his mom said, almost pleading. She was stuck on repeat, not knowing any other track. It was like she hoped this time would be the one he finally heard what she was trying to say. Scott did hear—he just didn't agree. Plenty of music artists were able to move seamlessly through the decades, their music adapting to the times.

"We make our own destinies." As soon as Scott said it, he knew it sounded like something you'd find on a cat poster.

"Scotty," his mom tried one more time, but her words faltered, and whatever she was going to say seemed to get stuck in her throat.

Scott's phone beeped with a new text. His ride was there. He stood from the couch and shoved the phone back into his pocket. "Matt and Jordan are out front—"

"They can wait," his dad said, a crispness to his tone. "We're not done here."

"But—"

His mom walked over and placed a hand on Scott's shoulder, her voice soft. "Listen to what he has to say." She pulled him so he sank onto the couch, but this time she sat with him, as if she were offering moral support.

Scott pulled his phone back out and shot a quick text, telling his friends to hold on a moment. Just as he tapped the send icon, his dad spoke.

"You're going away for the summer." His dad held up a hand, as if already anticipating the outburst Scott would have. Because there was no way there wasn't going to be an outburst—no way Scott was going to accept those six little words without a fight. "I've already talked to your manager, and it's worked out so your recording obligations will be finished before June, and I verified that you won't leave for your tour until Labor Day weekend."

"What, like bootcamp?" Scott asked, leaping back to his feet. "You can't send me away. I'll be eighteen."

"Not bootcamp," his mom said. "A summer job. It will be fun. Your last hurrah before going out into the world as an adult." She was trying to cajole him, make it seem like it was something other than the fact that they were sending him away. It was probably that thing where they dropped troubled kids in the middle of the desert and made them figure out how to survive.

Hurrah.

Scott snorted and folded his arms across his chest. "You haven't been able to make me go to school. What makes you think I'll agree to this?"

His dad also crossed his arms over his chest, matching Scott's stance. "Because you want control over your money. Your own life. This is how you're going to get it."

A sliver of panic rose in his chest. Could they do that? He'd thought once he turned eighteen, everything would turn over to him. "You can't do that. It's not legal."

"I'm currently a joint owner on your bank account. You need my signature for me to be removed from it."

Scott's mind raced. "But I can still take money out. I could remove all of it."

"Not when your account is frozen."

Scott's thoughts froze with it.

He didn't want to believe it possible, but his dad did manage a bank, and there was no way he'd do anything that could jeopardize his own career. His dad was a rule follower by nature and expected the same from Scott.

"Congratulations," Scott finally said, giving his dad the slow clap. "You've managed to take my assets hostage. You've become a real master manipulator, pulling one over on your teenage son. I bet you feel real good about yourself now."

His dad gave him a long stare, the hardness dissolving into something else indecipherable. Sadness, maybe. Except, Scott's dad didn't do sad. He did grumpy, angry, indifferent. But never sad. Until now.

"We just want what's best for you. Want you to rediscover who you are. Someone other than the rock star." His dad picked up a pamphlet from the table and walked it over to Scott. "It's only for ten weeks. If you stick it out, I'll sign everything you need."

Scott gave in to his curiosity and took the pamphlet from his dad. A montage of pictures was splayed across the front. Someone riding a zipline. Another person repelling over a cliff. Four-wheelers donned another page.

"What is this place?" It didn't seem like a survival camp.

"A dude ranch. A place where people can ride horses, get out in nature, stay in cabins," his mom said with a bright smile, though it seemed forced. "They've already told us they have a position for you. An activity guide. All you have to do is show up."

"A dude ranch. Tour guide by day, cow tipping by night."

Scott's dad threw him a wry smile. "Something like that."

Well, it could be worse. But he and his friends had plans. And they involved him not being sent away to learn to lasso.

"I'll think about it."

"Not much to think about."

Dreams of beach parties were quickly fading, being replaced by the image of him hot, sweaty, and alone in the middle of nowhere. Might as well be survival camp.

But his dad had made one thing clear.

Scott didn't have a choice.

"Fine. I'll go," he said. "But I'm not going to forget this—the ultimatum you've given me. That's not what parents do when they supposedly love their children."

Scott's phone chimed again, and a car horn blasted from the driveway. He didn't say goodbye to his parents this time or tell his mom not to wait up.

He didn't want anything to do with them right now. Not after what they'd done.

What he needed was a distraction. And Jordan and Matt were just the guys who could help him with that.

2

JULIANNA

F ree at last.

Julianna rolled her suitcase behind her as she exited the small airport in St. George, Utah. The doors automatically slid open in front of her, and the heat of the day crashed over her. She wished she hadn't stowed her baseball cap in her luggage.

A shuttle sat next to the curb a few yards to Julianna's right, the logo for Zion Ranch and Resort faded on the side. A smiling woman leaned against the side of it, her face tilted up to the sun, almost like she didn't care whether someone decided to hitch a ride or not. She was just enjoying the day.

Julianna pulled in a long breath. She could do this.

In spite of her family's expectations, she'd managed to make it all the way from Minnesota, and she hadn't freaked out once. Her parents had thought she'd make it as far as the end of the driveway before changing her mind.

No, she'd never been outside her small town, and certainly not by herself. Like her parents, she was a homebody. She liked comfortable. Predictable.

But there was nothing in Lakeview for Julianna. Along with comfortable and predictable, Julianna was also invisible.

And so she'd decided she was going to take control of her life —do something new and unexpected. It had been fate when Julianna had seen that post on her social media feed. A resort in Utah was hiring for the summer. You just had to be eighteen, which Julianna was—barely. Close enough that they'd hired her.

Ten weeks. Seventy days.

And they were going to be life changing.

They had to be, because she couldn't allow herself to go back to being invisible.

So, Julianna squared her shoulders, put on a smile that she hoped came across as confident, and walked up to the shuttle.

When the woman hadn't yet acknowledged Julianna, she tried for the classic clearing-the-throat routine, but it came out more like a hacking cough.

The woman started, her heel slipping off the curb, and she fell into the van's side.

"Are you okay?" Julianna asked, leaping forward to help.

The woman waved her off, laughing. "Yeah, yeah. Sorry, I got caught up in the moment. The clouds are beautiful today." She stole another glance, like she couldn't get enough.

Julianna didn't know the last time she'd taken a moment to look up at the sky, but when she tilted her face up, imitating the woman, all she got was a face full of sun, and she quickly shut her eyes.

The woman's eyes crinkled as she laughed. "Face this way." She circled her finger midair, indicating for Julianna to turn around so they were both looking in the same direction. "Now try again."

Julianna felt her cheeks warm with embarrassment, and she

really didn't care about the clouds anymore, but she did as the woman asked and looked up.

It was then that she understood why the woman hadn't wanted to look away.

"Wow," Julianna said softly. The sky looked like the type you only saw in movies, where the clouds were as puffy as cotton candy and appeared so close, you thought that if you just reached out far enough, you could touch them. Julianna leaned against the shuttle, imitating the woman. The clouds were moving surprisingly fast, and she wanted to ask them what their hurry was—why they couldn't stay a while longer.

It was the first time in months that she'd slowed down long enough to enjoy the moment—to feel at peace.

"Hello," a voice said.

It was much closer than Julianna would have expected, and she jumped. When her gaze whipped away from the clouds, she lost her balance—and fell into the shuttle. Just as the driver had done moments before.

"Sorry, didn't mean to scare you." A girl who looked maybe a year or two older than Julianna stood in front of them. She had wild mousy brown hair, freckles, and the most piercing green eyes that Julianna had ever seen. On top of all her frizz was a cowgirl hat. A plaid shirt and jeans completed the ensemble.

Julianna wondered if she was supposed to have all that stuff. She knew they were technically going to be working at a ranch, but it wasn't a real one. They just said that for marketing purposes. Real ranches didn't have places to get a massage, and they didn't make your bed each morning and leave a chocolate on your pillow.

"Nice hat," the driver said, then turned so she faced both girls. "You're my only travelers on this shuttle. The rest are either coming on the next one, or they procured their own way to the ranch." She held both arms out to her sides. "I'm Kat, short for Kassandra. Welcome to your first day of working at Zion Ranch and Resort."

"Isn't Kassie short for Kassandra?" the other girl asked, an eyebrow raised.

"If you're the type who likes the name Kassie." Kat leaned in close. "But I'm not that type." And then she straightened and released another round of infectious laughter. Julianna liked her already.

Kat placed a finger under her chin, and her gaze flitted between Julianna and the girl with the hat. "You must be Julianna," she said, pointing to the other girl.

"Nope, sorry. Penny." She extended a hand, and Kat shook it.

"Pleased to meet you. Short for Penelope, I'm assuming?"

Penny's lips tilted up on one side. "You'd think so, but my parents didn't want to take the chance that I'd actually want to go by my full name, so they went with the nickname from the get-go."

"Penny it is." Kat turned to Julianna. "Let me guess, you go by Julie."

"Nope, no nickname for me."

"Not even an occasional Jules?"

Julianna had never considered the need to shorten her name. Sure, it didn't roll off the tongue, but what was wrong with that? She liked her name. "Just Julianna."

Kat nodded, her eyes bright, like she suspected that would change by the end of the summer. "Okay, just Julianna, let's throw your suitcase in here and get on the road. Your journey today is not quite finished."

Kat opened up the back of the shuttle and placed both Penny and Julianna's luggage in, then ushered the girls through the side door.

As they buckled their seatbelts, Penny asked, "How far is it to the ranch?"

"An hour and a half. But it will go by quickly. We'll be driving through Zion National Park to get there, and if you've never seen it...well, you'll just have to experience it for yourselves."

"I've never been anywhere," Penny whispered, like it was a dark secret that she'd rather Kat not know about.

"Me neither," Julianna whispered back. And then they both laughed, like it was their own inside joke.

They leaned back into their seats, and Julianna released a contented sigh.

"Excited for the summer?" Kat asked, looking at the girls through her rearview mirror.

"Very," Penny and Julianna replied in unison. And then they laughed again.

And just like that, for the first time in four years, Julianna had made a friend.

"Wowza," Julianna said, stepping out of the shuttle. "This is... incredible." A giant three-story barn sat in front of them, a large field stretching out behind it. There weren't any cows, but there was a swimming pool. Julianna thought she'd probably enjoy that better.

"I know, right?" Kat bounded out from the driver's seat and opened the back door to the shuttle. "You'll get to explore all of it on your days off. As long as there are openings, you can join the guests on the activities."

Julianna took her suitcase from Kat. "What kinds of things do you have?" She knew they at least had a zipline because it had been featured on their website. Julianna tilted her head back until she saw it—at the top of the third story of the barn. It went over their heads and all the way into the middle of the field.

Penny followed her gaze. "That is really high." Her voice shook slightly, like she wasn't a fan of heights. Julianna didn't know if she was or not. She'd never had the chance to test it out.

"It's not so bad," Kat said, handing Penny her duffel bag. "But if you'd rather keep your feet on the ground, we have everything from shooting clay pigeons to four-wheeling. There's also rock climbing, repelling, archery, paintball, and of course hiking through Zion National Park."

"Oh, lovely," Penny said, though Julianna could have sworn that she was now three shades paler than she had been.

"If you look down that way, you'll see the stables." Kat pointed down a dirt road that led past the barn. "Because, seriously, what ranch would be complete without horseback riding?" Kat eyed Penny's cowgirl hat when she said it and gave her a friendly wink.

"Awesome." Penny's enthusiasm was nothing like what it had been on the drive over. It seemed forced, like maybe she hadn't realized what she was signing up for.

If Kat could tell how nervous Penny was, she didn't give any indication, instead rattling on like there was nothing out of the ordinary. "You both already received your assignments?"

Penny looked like she was still struggling to find her words, so Julianna spoke first. "I'm in the kid's camp." She didn't know what that was, but it sounded like it could be fun.

"Ooh, that's one of my favorite assignments in the place. Everyone always wants to be an activity guide, but I personally think the kids' camp is where it's at."

Julianna wondered if she should ask what that meant, but Kat's attention was pulled away by a man walking out from the barn. "Look at me, chattering away," Kat said, a lovely pink hue now tinging her cheeks. As if the man's presence had caused it.

Yes, he was good-looking, in a lumberjack kind of way, with his plaid shirt and the beginnings of a beard, but he also looked a bit gruff. Like she and Penny were just the beginning of many things on his to-do list. Maybe he was Kat's boss.

"The first to arrive," the man said, striding up. He smiled and stuck his hand out, his whole demeanor completely transformed. "I'm Jimmy, and I manage the activity barn, which means that if you are a guide, we'll be seeing a lot of each other over the next three months."

He looked between the two girls, as if waiting for them to confirm whether they were indeed activity guides.

"I'm in the kids' camp," Julianna finally said, partially raising her hand.

Jimmy gave a nod in her direction, but his gaze seemed stuck on Kat, who had taken a few steps back. "I'm not involved in the camp," he said, "but you will be housed on the second level of the activity barn, so we'll still pass each other from time to time." He managed to break his gaze away from Kat and turn his attention to Penny. "And where are you lucky enough to be this summer? Kids' camp as well?"

Penny seemed to have lost her voice, but after a moment of awkward silence, she said, "Um...no. I'll be an activity guide." She looked like she wanted to throw up at the admission.

Yikes.

Jimmy didn't seem to notice. Instead, his expression lit up. "That's wonderful. I look forward to working with you." His gaze returned to Kat. "We'll be having a good old-fashioned chuck-wagon dinner tonight to welcome everyone, but until then, Kassandra will help you find your bunk and get settled."

Kassandra? It was strange that he was so formal with a woman who clearly thrived on informal. If it bothered Kat, she didn't give any indication, though her smile may have momentarily dipped. It was difficult to tell because it had quickly returned, as big as ever. Too big.

Kat was about to say something, but her words were cut off by an approaching car. More like a boat, actually. And it was off-roading on the gravel, making its way to the barn.

"A limousine?" Penny squealed.

Okay, a limousine boat. There wasn't much difference in Julianna's mind.

Jimmy placed his hands on his hips and released a long sigh. "And so it begins." Rather than stick around to welcome the newcomer, he spun on one heel and quickly made his way back into the activity barn.

Kat seemed to feel the same sentiments as her co-worker and motioned for the girls to follow her. "Because you are first to arrive, you get first choice. Do you want to sleep on the second floor of the barn or underneath the lodge?" She nodded toward a long one-story building that bordered the swimming pool, then lowered her voice. "Just a word of advice—the apartment under the lodge has fewer girls, more privacy, and your own shower. But if you want to hike across the field and up the hill to use the guest showers, that's your call."

Julianna and Penny shared side glances, then laughed.

"The lodge sounds lovely," Penny answered.

Kat released a dramatic sigh. "I guess if personal amenities are your thing, I won't try to stop you." A grin then burst across her face. "Right this way."

Penny followed Kat, but the limousine was now parked in front of the barn, and Julianna hung back. What kind of person not only rode in a car like that to a dude ranch but then instructed their driver to take them off-roading in it? They really couldn't bother to walk from the parking lot down to the barn? It was like fifty yards.

Curious, Julianna slowed her steps and moved toward a low

wall that separated the gravel from the grass. She sat down and pretended to be insanely interested in the barn, and then the blue sky above her, which had considerably fewer clouds than earlier. Anything to not look like she was waiting to see who was going to step out of that limousine.

As it turned out, it was well worth the wait.

Scott stretched out in the back of the limo, watching the passing landscape. And to think his parents had wanted him to fly into St. George and take the shuttle from the airport like everyone else. Yeah, right. Once Scott had pointed out that he would be traveling alone and would most likely be in danger from all the crazy fans he seemed to attract, they agreed he should take the limo and driver that he usually used for special occasions—which turned out to be most weekends. When you were Scott Dallenforth, even a midnight run to the grocery store became a special occasion.

The car wound its way up a mountainous road, which Scott was sure Gerald didn't love, for forty-five minutes before the driver slowed and then turned under a large sign that said Zion Ranch and Resort. Scott suddenly felt queasy. He forced himself to draw slow breaths and run through exercises usually reserved for right before a big concert.

Why was he this nervous? It was only a few weeks in hickville. If he and his band could play in stadiums with thousands of screaming girls, security officers making sure they managed to get home in one piece, surely working a summer on a ranch would be a piece of cake. Sure, he'd probably have to pose for a few dozen pictures each day and sign some autographs. But it would be better than what he usually had to deal with. The owner of the ranch had assured his parents that the employees of Zion Ranch would be under strict rules to respect Scott's privacy.

The owner had said that just before he'd asked if Scott would be willing to play a concert at some point over the summer. Scott wasn't much without the rest of the band, but his parents had agreed to the concert. They hadn't asked Scott first, because they'd had all the details ironed out before he'd even known this place existed.

Some parents.

A tall barn came into view. A field. Horses. A swimming pool. What looked like one-room cabins dotted the landscape.

And people milling around. It looked like most, if not all, were employees. The queasiness returned. Maybe if Scott had Gerald drive close enough, he could slip straight from the limo to his accommodations without anyone seeing.

"Did my parents tell you who my point of contact is in this place?" Scott asked his driver.

"No, sir, but the resort does know to expect you at about this time."

If they did, they were keeping their word by not making a big deal out of his presence. No one so much as glanced at the limo as it lumbered past. Scott knew not to expect a parade, but this wasn't normal. The queasiness fled, leaving disappointment in its place.

"Drive down to that barn, Gerald. I'll find someone who can help us."

"The gravel doesn't seem like it's meant for driving on, sir."

"Come on, Gerald. Where's your sense of adventure? Besides, we have to find the guy who runs this place."

"It seems more likely that the owner of this establishment works from the lodge. Which doesn't require off-roading."

Gerald was a great guy, but he could be a bit of a stiff sometimes. Scott hated to pull out the *I'm the one who's paying you* card, but he really didn't want to be hauling his bags all over this place. "If you're worried about scratches on your car, you know that I'll have them fixed." Money wasn't an issue for Scott, not anymore. At least when these ten weeks were over with. And it was empowering.

"Very good, sir," Gerald said, though Scott could tell that the driver wanted nothing more than to park next to the lodge and throw Scott out with his luggage. Gerald pulled away from the road, and the limo bumped and slid along the gravel as they made their way to the barn. It was a lot bouncier than Scott had anticipated, and he considered the possibility that Gerald had been correct and off-roading in the limo might not have been the greatest idea.

Too late to turn back now, though. He'd finally attracted the attention of the ranch employees, and they watched as the limo moseyed its way over grass and gravel, and then to its final resting spot next to a low wall that bordered the barn. A girl sat on it, long blonde hair reaching the middle of her back and sunglasses perched a little too low on her nose. She was cute. Pretty, even. Maybe this wouldn't be such a bad summer.

Gerald stepped out and looked around, taking in the surroundings. His gaze seemed to settle on the girl for a moment too long—as if analyzing whether she was a threat—before he opened Scott's door for him.

A blast of heat replaced the perfectly controlled air of the limousine, and Scott joined Gerald. Placing his hands on his hips, he breathed in deeply. It wasn't a smell he was used to. Trees. Grass. Nature.

"Smell that, Gerald?"

The driver sniffed. "I'm not sure."

"Exactly. It's clean air." Scott reached into the back of the limo and grabbed a cowboy hat he'd made Gerald stop for on their way to Utah. It matched the plaid shirt and blue jeans he'd bought at the same time. Scott plopped the hat on his head. There. Ensemble complete. Now he would fit in with everyone else.

His gaze wandered back to the girl on the wall. She was now unabashedly staring, like she knew who he was but didn't know what to do with that information. So she'd just stare. It wouldn't be the first time, and it certainly wouldn't be the last.

Scott took a few steps toward her. "What do you think?" he asked her with a grin.

The girl's cheeks darkened and she whipped her head around, as if checking to see if there was anyone else he could possibly be talking to. She must have determined that he was indeed speaking to her, but she was still struggling with the whole creating sentences thing.

Finally, she managed, "Uh...yeah. Looks fine." She stumbled over her words, then fell silent again.

Scott's grin faded. "Only *fine*?"

"I meant good. Great, even," she said quickly.

"I'm just messing with you." His smile returned. It was so easy, he couldn't help teasing his fans. Scott turned back to Gerald. "Well, I guess I'll see you in ten weeks."

"You're sure this is a good idea?" Gerald asked, his lips pulled into a frown as he eyed the barn.

"Nope. But I don't have a choice. Mom and Dad said I need something to help me be more grounded. Frankly, I'm being held hostage. But I'm sure if I need anything, this lovely lady can help me out."

He winked in the girl's direction, and she looked like she might pass out.

Gerald cast a look in her direction that said he didn't trust her one bit, let alone think she'd be of any help to a famous rock star. "If you're sure," he said. After a couple more long looks, he removed Scott's luggage from the back, then got in the car, and the limo lumbered away.

Scott wanted to chase after Gerald and work out a deal where he'd drop Scott off in Vegas on his way back to California. Scott could lie low until Gerald returned for him.

But there was no way he'd be able to keep it secret for ten weeks—hotel staff were notorious for leaking who their famous guests were. And then his dad would never agree to unfreezing Scott's account. So, Scott tilted his cowboy hat back and studied the barn. Three levels. New paint job. Looked nice. "This is it. A dream come true. Always wanted to be a ranch hand." Not. But he had to keep up appearances. Could be great publicity. Make him seem down-to-earth, just like his parents wanted.

"You're not here as a guest?" the girl asked, though after she spoke, she looked like she wished she hadn't. In fact, she looked like she might throw up.

Scott tossed a smile in her direction. "Nope." His steps held a swagger as he walked toward her. "No one back home believed I was going to work on a real ranch. They don't think I will last a week before running back home. Of course, I'm just going to have to prove them wrong."

"Uh-huh," the girl said, her cheeks returning to their natural color. She no longer seemed nervous and was instead eying him with skepticism. "You know that it's a resort, right? It's not like an actual ranch."

Scott's smile slipped. "It is called Zion Ranch, correct?"

"Well, yes—"

"And I am currently standing next to a giant red barn, no?"

"Technically, that's true—"

Scott's grin returned, and he tipped his hat to the girl. "Then I think I just proved my point."

She looked like she didn't know what to do with him. Just as he liked it.

He held out his hand. "Scott...Andersen..." He wasn't sure why he'd just made up a name. There was no way she hadn't recognized him. Apparently the hat and plaid shirt wasn't as much of a disguise as he'd been hoping. To be fair, Gerald had warned him that that would be the case.

"Scott Andersen, huh?" The girl raised an eyebrow and studied him, as if staring long enough would help everything suddenly make sense. "Julianna Barrow." She took his hand but only held it briefly before letting go. She gave him a placating smile and said, "Welcome to Zion Ranch, cowboy."

"Ranch hand. I still have to learn to rope steer before I can call myself a true cowboy." He said it as if this were the most natural thing in the world. Scott couldn't help himself. There was something about this girl that made him want to tease her. Rile her up. Maybe it was because she gave such good reactions, and he wanted to see what she'd do next. "Oh, and I'm going to call you Jules, if you don't mind. It suits you better."

That did it—got just the reaction Scott had been hoping for. The girl looked incredulous, like she didn't know if she wanted to strangle Scott or get him to kiss her.

"Julianna, where'd you end up?" someone called from over by the lodge. A girl with crazy curly hair appeared around a corner. And she wore a cowgirl hat.

"Look." Scott pointed to the girl, who had promptly stopped

mid-step. "I'm not the only one in a hat and plaid. That's what
people wear when they work on a ranch." Scott *tsked* and
stepped back while folding his arms over his chest. "You're never
going to make it through the summer."

Julianna's lips twitched like she was trying not to smile, and
she crossed her arms, mirroring Scott. "Yeah, well, I don't
remember there being many limos on a ranch either."

Touché.

"How about this?" he said. "We call a truce. You teach me
everything you know about roping cattle, and I'll teach you
everything I know about...everything else."

Julianna stared, like she was trying to figure out if he was
joking or not. "You do know that there aren't actually cows at
this place, right? Like, zero."

Hmm. What he'd seen on the brochure the day his parents
had roped him into this mess was the extent of his knowledge,
and he swore there had been cattle on the front page of the
brochure. "Yeah, of course," he said with a laugh. "I was just
messing with ya."

Julianna's lips did that twitching thing again. "You brought a
lasso, didn't you?"

"I—what—of course not—" Scott's gaze jumped to his suitcase, then back to Julianna, who wasn't even trying to hide her
smirk now. "Yeah. I brought a lasso."

"Maybe we can find a bale of hay for you to practice on. Just
in case. You never know when a skill like that will come in
handy. Maybe when all the girls go crazy fangirl, you could use
it for self-protection."

Scott's face was burning from embarrassment, and the curly
haired girl had apparently gotten over her shock and was now
approaching them. His gaze bounced around wildly. Where was
a welcoming committee when he needed one? Shouldn't

someone be showing him the layout of the place, telling him where he could stow his bags and all that?

As if on cue, a man exited the barn and walked toward them, though he didn't seem at all excited by the prospect.

Scott was having serious doubts about anyone going crazy fangirl on him.

It seemed no one wanted him there in the first place.

4

JULIANNA

"I can't believe you were just talking with Scott Dallenforth," Penny said, not even bothering to lower her voice as they walked toward the lodge. "No wonder you got sidetracked. Bet you wish we were sleeping in the barn now. That's where all the boys stay." She must have seen Julianna's shocked expression because she hurriedly added, "Not in the same space as the girls, of course."

Julianna glanced over her shoulder, hoping that Scott hadn't heard anything. He had a big enough ego as it was, he didn't need to think girls were fawning over him already. And trying to figure out how they could sleep as close to him as possible.

"The more distance, the better," Julianna said, hooking her arm through Penny's.

"I don't suppose he's working as an activity guide, is he?" Penny asked it as if she hadn't even heard Julianna. "Maybe he can catch me when I fall off the rock wall."

Of course Penny would be interested in the rock star. Hadn't her own heart beaten faster than it should have? Hadn't her thoughts jumped to all the places that Penny's were?

Which was why Julianna had to stay away.

People like Scott Dallenforth were better as a poster on her wall, never knowing how long she stared at them, wishing for things that could never be.

Okay, that thought came out really creepy, and she was glad it had stayed in her head. But guys like him had too much attention for their own good. And the more girls threw themselves at them, the worse it got.

Julianna wasn't going to be a part of the problem. And she wasn't going to be Scott's personal ranch tutor.

"You know why he was acting like that, don't you?" Julianna asked as they walked toward the lodge. "Pretending he needs me to teach him a thing or two. Because I wasn't falling at his feet like everyone else does. Once he gets a reaction, he'll be on to the next girl. Because that's what guys like him do. He didn't stop to think what it does to girls like me—girls who haven't had a date in two years. The boy probably has a date every night of the week, including school nights—"

"What are you talking about?" Penny interrupted. They were standing at the top of a stairway that led down under the lodge, and she was staring at Julianna like she'd lost her mind.

"Um..."

"Wait, did you and Scott have a *moment*?"

Julianna snorted, like that was the most ridiculous thing in the world. Because it was. It had to be. She lifted her suitcase and walked down the stairs, leaving Penny no choice but to follow her. "Of course not. The boy wouldn't know a 'moment' if it smacked him upside the head. Do you realize that he actually brought a lasso? Thought he'd be roping steer or something ridiculous like that."

"I brought a lasso."

Julianna stopped at the bottom of the stairs. They were standing in what looked like a long window well, a narrow passageway stretching in front of them. To their left were three doors. She glanced over her shoulder, taking in Penny's hat and plaid shirt. And how her smile had dipped. Like Julianna's words had hurt her.

"I-I'm sorry, I didn't mean it like that," Julianna said, stumbling over her words, but Penny held up a hand, stopping her from saying more.

"Yes. You did." Penny released a sigh. "Look, when you're traveling across the country to work at a dude ranch, it's only natural to have some fun with it. Maybe you're just looking for something to be wrong with Scott." Penny brushed past Julianna and entered the second door.

Maybe Penny was right. But then Julianna thought of the limo and the chauffeur and how Scott was already acting like he owned the place.

There was no way that Scott Dallenforth was the down-to-earth guy that Penny wanted him to be.

When Julianna entered the apartment, she paused. Like the outside corridor, it was long and narrow, bunk beds lining two walls. Past them was an open bathroom, and beyond that the laundry machines.

"This is..." Julianna paused when Penny threw her a curious glance, maybe wondering if Julianna was going to find something wrong with their living arrangement as well. So much for making a friend. "This is awesome. Seriously, it's going to be like a party every night. Except with no parents telling us to go to bed." At least Julianna assumed that was what parties were like. She wouldn't know.

She must have got it right, though, because Penny brightened, and a grin split across her face. "Absolutely. I wonder what the other girls will be like. Cool, I bet. How could you choose to work at a place like this and not be cool? What do you want to do on your first day off? I was thinking that shooting at clay pigeons could be fun, but maybe we should go hiking instead. You know, something that isn't going to get us killed."

Penny kept talking as she threw her duffel bag onto one of the top bunks, but then abruptly stopped, and her gaze landed on Julianna. "Do you snore?"

"I...don't think so."

"You should sleep on this top bunk by me, then. I don't think I could handle sleeping right next to a snorer."

Julianna hesitated. She hadn't slept on a top bunk since she was six—when she'd fallen off during the night and broken her arm.

Unfortunately, Penny misinterpreted her silence, and her smile faded. "Or not. That's cool." And then she turned away.

Julianna squeezed her eyes shut. She could do this. "I'm afraid of bunk beds." The words exploded out, leaving her feeling vulnerable.

When she opened her eyes again, she found Penny watching her. "You mean, you're afraid of heights?"

"No, not heights. At least I don't think so. I'm not completely sure." She gave a quick shake of her head. "Just bunk beds. I don't like that I'm asleep on a platform and have no control whether I toss and turn and could fall and..." Her words trailed off, and she wished she could backtrack and make herself seem less pathetic than she already felt.

Penny shrugged, not seeming the least bit fazed. "That's cool. Why don't you take the bottom, then? We'll interrogate other potential roomies to weed out those who could be a problem."

Julianna stared, then laughed. Who was this girl? Every time she spoke, she managed to catch Julianna off guard. "You want to interrogate the other girls?"

"Absolutely. I mean, I know I said everyone here is probably going to be cool, but even cool people have sinus issues."

The door to their basement apartment opened, and two girls entered.

Julianna's breath caught in her chest. No, no, no, no. This wasn't happening. She had come all the way from Minnesota with the sole purpose of getting away from girls like these.

No, not girls *like* these. These girls, specifically.

"Let's skip the interrogation and just assume that they snore," Julianna whispered, turning away and tossing her bag onto the bunk under Penny's.

"Both of them?" Penny asked, an eyebrow raised. Her gaze swept over the girls, like she was trying to see what Julianna obviously did.

"Yup. Definitely snorers."

The girls placed their bags down and looked around the room. "What do you think?" one of them asked. "Better than the barn?"

Amanda. Crazy rich and popular. Not someone Julianna really wanted to bunk with.

"Definitely. There were like fifty beds up there, and no bathroom."

And Sandra. Someone Julianna wanted to bunk with even less. She was still sporting her spiked bracelets and skull T-shirt, even on a dude ranch.

Amanda laughed. "Let's claim our bunks and then go take a million pictures that we can send to Gracie and Alexis. They're going to be so bummed they chose to stay behind."

"We can try, but I doubt they'll care much when they have things like boyfriends and medical school." A pause. "Hey, I think I recognize that girl."

Oh, no. The last thing that Julianna needed was for Sandra to try to make conversation. Julianna sat on her bed and busied herself with her suitcase.

"Yeah," Amanda said. "She goes to our school, right?"

"Crazy how we ended up working the same summer job."

Julianna glanced over her shoulder. Yes, it was amazing that they had all ended up at the same dude ranch thousands of miles from home.

Which could only mean one thing.

Her mother's book club.

Her mom had probably been venting about Julianna leaving home for the summer. She had been worried about Julianna being so far from home, considering she'd never been away from her parents for longer than a weekend.

And apparently, instead of being dissuaded from signing their daughters up, the other mothers had thought it was a pretty great idea.

"You know those girls?" Penny asked, though she was kind enough to keep her voice low. Her gaze flitted between Julianna and the girls still standing by the front door.

"You could say that. We went to the same school." Of course, no one could ever infiltrate Amanda and Sandra's little clique, so Julianna wouldn't go so far as to say that she knew them. And what little Julianna did know, she wished she didn't. "Hopefully there aren't any other surprises."

The door opened again.

"Hey, this place is way nicer than ours." A low voice. And a familiar one.

Julianna couldn't help herself. She spun toward the door. Blair. Sandra's boyfriend. And the boy Julianna had been in love with for three years. A swimmer. Well built. Funny. And when they'd been assigned as partners on a school project, she'd actually thought she'd had a chance.

Instead, he'd gone for the goth chick.

Blair's best friend, Cameron, stuck his head around the corner. He was dating Amanda.

This just kept getting worse.

"Hey, you can't be in here," Sandra said, though she was laughing while she attempted to push the boys back out. She wasn't trying very hard.

"Better than being around that Scott guy. What's he playing at, coming here and pretending like he's normal? No one is buying it."

Sandra stopped pushing. "What Scott guy?"

"You know, that singer? Can't remember the name of the band, but half the girls at school had a picture of them hanging in their lockers."

Not only had Sandra stopped trying to get rid of the boys, but Amanda had actually pulled them into the apartment. "You are not saying that Scott Dallenforth is a guest at this ranch," she said, though she looked like she wouldn't accept any other answer.

"No, he's not a guest here," Blair said. But before anyone had the chance to be disappointed, he continued. "He's working here, same as us."

And then, despite the fact that both girls had boyfriends, they abandoned their bags and rushed outside, leaving the two boys exchanging confused looks.

Blair glanced in Penny and Julianna's direction and started, like he was just now noticing there was anyone else there. That was no surprise, considering Blair had rarely noticed Julianna through the nine years they had gone to school together.

Why should now be any different?

"Oh, hey," he said, like he knew who she was but was trying to recall her name. "I hadn't realized you'd be working here too."

Cameron spun around, like he was trying to figure out who his friend was talking to.

Bitter feelings of rejection washed over Julianna, the old painful memories resurfacing. She shoved them back down and forced a smile. "Yeah. Crazy, right?"

Blair threw a beautiful smile her way. "The craziest."

Penny was glancing between the two like she was trying to figure out what was going on. After a moment she gave up and instead crossed her arms over her chest and gave the boys a pointed look. "I hate to break it to you, but this is a *girls'* apartment. And I know it sucks that your girlfriends, or whoever they are, just abandoned you for a hot rock star. But this is kind of—"

"Yeah, yeah, we get it. Not allowed in your sacred place," Cameron interrupted. "We'll go back to our barn now." His lips dipped, like he wasn't thrilled about the prospect.

"Say hi to Scott for us," Penny called after their retreating backs. And then she turned to Julianna. "Okay, that whole... thing...was weird." She jumped onto her bed and crossed her legs, her expression eager. "Spill."

5

SCOTT

Despite the fact that Scott had been strong-armed into working at Zion Ranch, he'd found a silver lining to the whole thing. For the first time since he and his bandmates had been discovered in that local garage band competition, he'd be able to pretend he had a normal life. Yes, he was missing out on going to Cabo with his best friends, but it wasn't like he hadn't been before. Matt and Jordan would probably spend the whole month drunk and wouldn't remember it anyway.

Scott had sometimes wondered what it would be like to be a normal guy—work at a summer job and hang out for a few months without all the pressures of his rock-star lifestyle. Not often, of course. It hadn't taken him long to get used to fame and the special treatment that came with it. But on occasion, he wondered what life would be like if he decided to walk away from it all.

After less than twenty-four hours, he had his answer. It turned out he couldn't go back to being normal.

Instead, Scott had never felt lonelier. When the other guys at the ranch found out who they were rooming with, they immediately distanced themselves. Some appeared to be intimidated, sending smiles his way even as they chose bunks on the opposite end of the large room. And then there were those who didn't even pretend to like him. That mostly had to do with their girlfriends. Nothing personal, Scott tried to tell himself.

He was relieved when he walked into the lodge the next morning for breakfast and saw the blonde girl he'd met when he'd first arrived. She was sitting at a table by herself. Scott couldn't remember her name, but at least he'd have one friendly person to eat with. Except, by the time he'd gotten through the cafeteria-like line and approached her table, another girl was sliding into the spot next to her.

Scott tried to make it seem like he was just walking past, but the curly haired girl caught his eye and smiled. "Hey, Scott Dallenforth. Come sit with us." She patted the empty space next to her.

Another byproduct of fame. He was never just Scott. It was like people thought if they didn't use his last name, he wouldn't know they were talking to him. Or maybe they thought they weren't allowed—like only his friends and family were on a first-name basis with the star.

The blonde girl didn't look so eager to have him eat with them. In fact, she looked panicked, like she'd prefer anyone else sit with them. Anyone but him. Disappointment settled in his stomach.

Scott was about to decline when he noticed every other girl in the room watching him, their gazes predatory.

"Thank you," he said, and slid in opposite the blonde girl. Her name started with an L, he thought. Maybe a J. Jessica? Julie? Yeah, he thought it was that last one. Scott remembered now. She'd liked it when he'd called her Jules. He threw her a smile as he cut into his sausage. "Hey, Jules. How'd you sleep? Dream about anything exciting?"

She blinked, apparently too stunned to answer. Or do

anything else, for that matter. A half-eaten pancake sat on her plate, her fork in hand but hanging limply, like she'd forgotten what she was doing with it.

"I slept great," the curly haired girl said when the silence became too stifling. She threw a pointed glance at her friend, who still hadn't said anything. At one point, Jules's lips moved, but nothing came out. "I'm Penny, by the way." She stuck out her hand, and Scott shook it. It was sticky. Hopefully from syrup.

"Hi, Penny." He shoved a forkful of sausage into his mouth, then said, "What's wrong with her?" He pointed his fork at Jules.

Penny lifted a shoulder. "Don't know. She was fine until you showed up." And then she busied herself with what was left of her pancake. "But that's not saying much. I think that's probably true of everyone here."

Scott wondered what Penny meant by that, but before he had the chance to ask, Jules spoke up.

"It's Julianna."

He had just shoved a large piece of hash browns into his mouth, and he nearly choked on it. "Sorry?"

Even though Jules had seemed to find her voice again, she seemed flustered, and she wouldn't look at him. Her gaze remained on her plate when she said, "It's Julianna. My name. Not Jules."

Scott raised an eyebrow. "Why?"

She still wouldn't look at him. "That's what my parents named me."

Nobody was so uptight that they didn't appreciate a good nickname, and she certainly hadn't seemed it yesterday. In fact, Scott would go so far as to say that they had had a nice flirting session. They might have even had a "moment."

So, what had happened between yesterday and today?

That was when Scott noticed her gaze flicking between him and a group that sat on the other side of the room. Two couples who were obviously dating, considering they couldn't seem to keep their hands off each other.

Was that why she was mad? Was Jules expecting that of him? Maybe she'd misunderstood and thought because they had flirted a little the day before, they would suddenly be one of those couples.

He'd just been having a little fun, but that was the problem. Scott could never just have fun. If he gave a girl too much attention or went on more than one date with her, she expected things of him.

"I'm sorry, I think this was a bad idea. Sorry to bother you." Scott slid out from the table and carried his tray to where a dishwasher was collecting them. He tried to ignore Jules's surprised expression.

It wasn't just sitting next to her for breakfast that had been the bad idea.

It had been coming down to the ranch at all.

THE FIRST STAFF meeting of the summer. Yay.

Jimmy, who was apparently the activities manager, leaned against the checkout desk in the barn. As the name implied, it was where guests could get equipment or sign up for activities. His gaze swept over the group gathered in front of him. It wasn't just the activity guides who were there, but also housekeepers, maintenance...anyone who was there for the summer.

"Look around," Jimmy said. "These are your new best friends. You are going to eat together, work together, play together, sleep together..." He frowned as chuckles rippled through the group. "Not like that. You know what I mean. If y'all aren't getting along, then everyone else has to suffer. So...we are going to get to know each other in the best way I know how. A six-hour hike."

If this had been back home, that announcement would have been accompanied by a collective groan. Luckily Scott stopped himself just before his own groan escaped. Here, with all these people who had actually chosen to come work on a ranch, excited chatter broke out. It was like these people couldn't think of anything more fun than literally wandering around the middle of nowhere. Hungry. Sweaty. Tired. Sore. That was what apparently equated to a good time around here.

"And yes, before anyone asks, you will be paid for it. We take our guests on guided hikes, and so you need to be familiar with Zion National Park's unique terrain."

More excited chatter.

"Go fill up your water bottles in the cafeteria, make sure you are wearing proper footwear and have sunscreen, and I will meet you back here in thirty minutes."

Scott thought there were probably worse things than being paid to go hiking, but he couldn't think of what. It wouldn't be so bad if he were going with people he liked. And who liked him back.

This?

This was going to be six hours of torture, trying to avoid the attention of the girls while at the same time the daggers from the guys. There was no way this thing was going to have a happy ending.

It wasn't that he thought he was particularly attractive. Or that his personality was any more charming than the next guy.

But he was Scott Dallenforth, and being famous had changed things, both for good and bad. Would he ever wish to go back to how it had been?

Nope.

As annoying as situations like these were, he would never give up that feeling he had when he was on stage. All the lights on him as he did what he loved best, with the people he loved best.

He wouldn't give up a thing.

Which meant that it was time he stopped tiptoeing around everyone.

It was time for Scott Dallenforth to just be himself, whatever the consequences. It might lead to a few broken hearts and a couple of angry guys, but hey, that was nothing new for him.

Just another day in the life of a rock star.

So, with new resolve, he tightened his brand-new hiking shoes, only worn once. He then filled up his water bottle, stuck on a baseball hat, and planned on having the best hike of his life.

At least, that was what he told himself. Until they were descending the trail that led into a slot canyon and Jules appeared at his side. She looked amazing, her long hair pulled up into a ponytail and sunglasses accentuating her features. Even her jeans and T-shirt seemed to have the one job of making her look good.

"I'm sorry," she said, skipping any pleasantries. "This morning. I was rude."

Scott kept his gaze on the trail, trying to play it cool. "Does that mean I can call you Jules?"

Her lips twitched up. "No."

"I might anyway."

"I won't answer."

Scott fought a smile. He didn't know why it was such a big deal to her. Or to him, for that matter. He knew he should respect her wishes, but she just didn't seem like a Julianna to him. When he thought of her, he saw the teasing smile she had worn the day before and not the stiff frown of that morning.

"If it means that much to you, I won't call you Jules. To your face."

"I suppose that's something."

They walked in silence before Scott got up the courage to ask, "Is that why you were distant this morning? Because of the name thing?" He usually never cared what girls thought of him, but he found himself hoping that that was all it had been—her being annoyed by a nickname.

She hesitated. "No." She paused before rushing on. "If I'm being completely honest here, I'm not the kind of girl that rock stars talk to, let alone eat breakfast with. I'm the nobody in the corner. If you're looking for an ego trip—someone to tell you how amazing you are while sneaking pictures when they think you're not looking—I'm not your girl. Not to mention the fact that you're totally messing with my groove."

Scott stumbled on a rock on the trail and Jules grabbed his arm, helping stabilize him. She let go just as quickly.

"Your...what?"

"You know, my groove? My mojo?" She made a hand sign that looked like she might be trying to be a gangster, but a really terrible one. Scott bit back a smile as Jules raised a shoulder, no longer in gangster stance. "It's hard enough for someone like me to make friends. And if you are sitting across from me at breakfast or acting like we're close...or something...it only makes things that much harder. They'll see me as competition, even if I'm not." Her words stopped as quickly as they had started. Like it hadn't been something she'd wanted to admit. Especially aloud.

"You have Penny," he pointed out.

Jules paused as she considered that. "Yes, I do." She looked around. "Speaking of, where is she?"

Scott spotted Penny's curly hair up at the front of the group. She appeared to be trying to jump while clicking her ankles together, but because of the steep decline, she kept stumbling forward, then laughing uncontrollably.

When Scott pointed her out, Jules said, "She has such an infectious personality." Her tone was sadder than Scott would have expected. "She's one of the nicest people I've ever met, and everyone is drawn to her."

"And...is that a bad thing?"

"No. It's just...I guess I wish I could be like that." She released a small sigh. "Sorry, sometimes I say too much. And really, I'm talking more to myself than to you. It helps me process my thoughts." Jules glanced around, like she was suddenly uncomfortable. "I'm...going to walk somewhere else now."

"Wait." Scott grabbed Jules's hand before she could hurry off. He hadn't meant to, but now that he had, he realized how nice hers felt in his. It had been a long time since he'd held a girl's hand. Scott had lost count of how many girls he had locked lips with, and the sad thing was, even though it was fun, he no longer felt anything when kissing someone. It wasn't special anymore.

But holding hands—that was about connection. Intimacy. He dropped Jules's hand.

She folded her arms over her chest, like she wanted to make sure he didn't grab her hand again. But she didn't seem mad. Instead, her gaze was curious.

"What?" she asked when Scott didn't say anything. "Why did you ask me to wait?"

How could he tell her that he felt as lonely as she did? That he wanted to connect with people in a way that wasn't fake? Like he could with her.

But he didn't. Because he was too much of a coward to actually get real with someone.

"Who were those people you kept looking at during breakfast?" he asked instead.

Jules's expression turned panicked, and her gaze darted

around, like she wondered if the people from breakfast were listening in. "No one." And then she hurried down the hill.

She was promptly replaced by several other girls vying for his attention, but Scott barely registered their presence.

Because the one person he wanted to spend a six-hour hike with wanted nothing to do with him.

6

JULIANNA

"They never said we would be hiking through a river," Julianna said, her arms out to her sides as if she were a tightrope walker. "I mean seriously, this is crazy."

Penny was just in front of her and slipped, barely catching herself before falling. "I feel like we're walking over waxed bowling balls."

That was an accurate way to describe it. They had descended into a slot canyon, the walls looming high above them, and a river at the bottom replacing the smooth trail they'd started out on. The high canyon walls blocked out much of the sun, and water had worn down the rocks so well that they were completely smooth. Great for the rocks. Not so great for anyone trying to walk over them. After thirty minutes of hiking on an actual trail, it had turned into this.

A large splash exploded from behind them, followed by gasps and laughter. Looked like someone had finally succumbed to the bowling balls. When Julianna glanced back to see who it was, guilt settled over her.

Scott sat in the water, spluttering, his face contorted in pain. But no one was helping him. Instead, because he was who he was, everyone had pulled their phones out of their waterproof bags and were taking pictures. Okay, maybe not everyone. Sandra, Amanda, Blair, and Cameron weren't. Julianna had to give them credit for that. But they seemed conflicted about whether they should approach the rock star to help. Like they wondered if they were allowed to. Maybe others were having the same thoughts. Like the guy was untouchable.

Anger replaced Julianna's guilt, and she wished Jimmy and Kat hadn't handed out those waterproof bags. Everyone's phones being ruined would have been better than letting them take advantage of someone else's misfortune.

Her mind made up, Julianna turned and made her way to Scott as quickly as possible—which wasn't at all fast. As she stumbled along, she called, "Break it up, people. If I see any of those pictures show up online, I will personally throw your phones off the top of the barn."

Julianna thought Scott would be grateful for her standing up for him. The look he threw her said otherwise.

"How funny is she?" Scott asked, his lips quirking up into a half-smile as he attempted to stand. He lost his balance and fell again, resulting in more pictures from the gathered group. "I don't mind a few pictures. In fact, make sure to tag me in them." He threw another smile as he finally regained his balance.

Assuming that the show was over, the group turned to resume the hike, and he promptly fell again.

Now Julianna didn't know who she was angrier with, the people taking the pictures or Scott. When she finally reached him, she stuck out a hand. "You look like you could use some help."

"No thank you." He ignored her hand and made another attempt at standing. Which failed.

"Why are you acting like this?"

Guilt flashed across his face, but it was quickly gone. "Like what?"

"Like what they were doing was okay? Taking pictures so they can throw them on social media or sell them to the press, without even trying to help. And then you rejected the one person who acts like they care."

Scott glanced around, as if making sure no one was watching. "Fine." He stuck his hand out, and she helped him up.

"Oh my gosh, you are freezing," she said. Scott's hand was ice-cold from his multiple attempts at pushing himself off the rocks. Without asking, she wrapped his hands in hers and rubbed them. "What they did, it wasn't right."

Scott was studying Julianna, his expression indecipherable. And yet it made Julianna's heart pick up speed. Left her breathless.

He glanced away. "I know. But in my line of work, appearances are everything. And if people see I can laugh it off when I fall down and make a fool of myself, it makes me more likable. If I'm mad that no one cares that I just bruised my tailbone and it hurts to walk, then I come across as a jerk."

Julianna shook her head. She didn't understand show business. And she really didn't want to. But she also saw that Scott was more complex than she had wanted him to be. It was easier when she saw him as a spoiled rock star who expected everything to be handed to him.

"You good?" she asked, opening her hands so Scott could remove his.

He didn't move.

"They're warm, thank you. But," he paused, "would you mind not letting go? I'm serious about the bruised tailbone, and I'm not sure if I can walk on my own. I know you don't want people to think we're friends...or more than friends...but I'd rather people see us holding hands than me using you as a human crutch."

Julianna didn't know how she felt about that. Oh, she certainly wouldn't mind holding Scott's hand for the next few hours. In fact, she would enjoy it. A lot. But it would also make her a target and ensure that she wouldn't make another friend the rest of her time at the ranch.

"It's selfish, I know," Scott said quickly. "We both have an image to keep, and it's not fair for me to ask you to give up yours."

Julianna hadn't thought of it like that—like she was trying to appear as something other than what she was. Hadn't she been angry with the others who had just watched Scott when he fell, not offering to help? Were those really the type of people she wanted to be friends with?

She already knew the answer. Julianna couldn't allow herself to do the same—to refuse help to someone who needed it.

Even if it was Scott Dallenforth.

Julianna hesitated, then reached out and interlocked her fingers with his.

"I guess physical coordination isn't a requirement for being a rock star?" she teased, trying to distract herself from her quickening heart rate. She could already feel her hands getting sweaty.

Scott snorted and threw her a dimpled grin. "No one can be coordinated in this insanity." He held her gaze for a moment before pink tinged his cheeks and he turned away. Julianna didn't have time to decipher what the reaction could have meant because Scott's gaze landed somewhere ahead, and he groaned. "Oh, great. Just what I need."

Up ahead, the river dropped over a wall of rocks, and the rest of the group was taking turns sliding down a boulder that was about as tall as Julianna. Jimmy and Kat were standing at the bottom, assisting and making sure everyone got down safely.

"It's fine. We'll slide down together."

Even though they were already moving at a snail's pace, Scott somehow managed to walk even slower. "They're going to get more pictures," he said, his voice soft. Julianna was unsure if the words were meant for her, but she couldn't help but feel sympathy for Scott. As tough as he tried to act, as much as he pretended that he hadn't been bothered by everyone's actions earlier, the look in his eyes told a different story.

Right now, Scott wanted to be anywhere but here.

"Let's not give them the chance."

Scott's eyebrow rose. "What do you mean?"

"Let's just wait for a few minutes. Wait until everyone has already gone ahead a bit, and then I'll help you down."

He hesitated, like he was unsure if he was okay with having to rely on Julianna—possibly afraid that someone would see. But he ultimately agreed. When Jimmy and Kat had helped the last person in front of them, Scott told them he needed to sit down for a moment but they'd catch up.

Jimmy gave his head a vigorous shake. "No way. I'm not about to lose one of our employees. And frankly, you'd be the worst one to lose."

Scott scowled, making him look like the spoiled celebrity he probably was, but Jimmy didn't seem to care, and he didn't back down.

Time for Julianna to turn on the charm—not that she'd had much practice. It couldn't hurt to try, though. "He injured himself on the rocks back there. Can't he have just a minute?" Her tone was ridiculously sweet, and she attempted to dial it back a notch. "I don't think his parents, or the media, would appreciate if he were injured even worse because you pushed him beyond what he should do."

Scott turned his scowl on Julianna, and she wondered if she'd made a mistake by interfering again. He never seemed to appreciate her efforts. But he needed to finish this hike, and he didn't want anyone else to see her help him down this rock. What else was she supposed to do?

"I can hang back with them," Kat said, placing a hand on Jimmy's arm. "Why don't you go ahead with the others?"

Apparently the rest of the group wasn't even aware that their fearless leaders were absent, because they were already nearly around the next bend.

Jimmy released an annoyed breath but said, "Fine. Don't take too long, though. I don't like when the group is separated."

And then Jimmy hurried to catch up with the others at a surprisingly quick pace, considering the slick rocks that had been giving everyone else trouble.

As soon as he disappeared around the bend with the others, Kat said quietly, "Which is hurt worse? You or your ego?" She didn't sound like she was trying to be mean but like she really wanted to know if he was hurt.

"Both," Scott said. When Kat raised a skeptical eyebrow, he folded his arms across his chest. "I'm serious. It hurts to walk. I'm pretty sure I bruised up my arms and legs trying to get back up." He pulled in a long breath. "But if we're being honest here, I can only afford one screwup a day. One fall is endearing. Multiple falls get me labeled as the rock star that must have been drunk when he went on the hike because he couldn't stay on his feet. There's a very thin line between reality and what the media will label me as."

Julianna hadn't spent much time with Scott, but even in this short amount of time, she realized how exhausting his life must be. She couldn't imagine having to be so aware of what others' perceptions of you were all the time. Julianna had thought it bad that everyone always ignored her. But maybe being invisible wasn't all that bad.

Kat nodded slowly, like she understood his perspective. "Let's get you down here and then I have to catch up to the group. I'll come back and check on you every so often to make sure you're doing okay—I can't have you lagging too far behind." She turned to Julianna. "It's easier with two people. Mind joining me?"

Julianna slid down the slick rock, Kat catching her around the waist and slowing her descent. When she splashed at the bottom, Julianna felt invigorated, almost like she'd just got a kick of adrenaline. That showed how many adventurous things she'd done in her life. She realized she needed to do more because she loved this feeling and wanted to know where she could get more of it.

Scott seemed less sure about sliding down, but with both Julianna and Kat catching him, he reached the bottom unscathed and still standing.

"Remember, don't get too far behind. Can't have an international incident on our hands, right?" And then Kat moved up the river, not waiting for an answer.

As soon as she was gone, Julianna laughed. "Hear that? You are an international incident."

Scott didn't answer right away, instead taking her hand like it was the most natural thing in the world and beginning to move up river. "My mom is always telling me that I need to plan my life as if my success won't last. Like it could all be taken away tomorrow. That's why I'm here. She wants me to remember what it was like before all"—he waved a hand through the air—"this."

Julianna felt Scott lose his footing, and she tightened her grip, steadying him. "You don't want to be here?"

"Nope. I was given an ultimatum." He threw a curious glance her way. "Why are *you* here?"

Julianna hesitated. She liked talking about Scott and his issues more than her own. When he finally nudged her in the side, reminding her that she was expected to answer the question, she threw him a smile. "Because I wanted to learn to use a lasso. Same as you."

Scott gave a single, loud "Ha!" that he morphed into a smaller chuckle. "Liar. We both know that you're already an expert. You promised to teach me, remember?"

"I believe I was volunteered for the position."

He raised a shoulder. "Same difference." He then got quiet and asked, "No, seriously. What brought you here? You and Penny thought you'd come and do something exciting before heading off to college or something?"

"I didn't come with anyone, same as you. Didn't meet Penny until yesterday."

Scott's lips parted in surprise. "Oh. You two get along so well, I just assumed."

Julianna smiled at the thought. "Penny's awesome, and I'm lucky to be bunking with her. I just... I don't make friends so easily."

Scott was quiet, like he was thinking, before he snapped his fingers. "Those people at breakfast. At the next table over. You acted like you knew them. See? You got friends."

She snorted. If he only knew. "Um...no. Those were not my friends."

"That's too bad. Though I can't say you're missing out on much. Those guys keep thinking I'm here to steal their girlfriends. As if. I'm not really into the skulls and crossbones thing, you know?"

Julianna couldn't tell if Scott was just trying to make her feel better or not, because really, Sandra was gorgeous, goth vibe aside. She appreciated the effort, all the same.

Except, that did give her an idea. A way for Blair to finally notice Julianna.

"Are you sure you aren't into goth girls? Because she isn't the type to worship vampires or anything. Although she's really into something called Day of the Dead, so not completely clear on that."

Flashbacks hit Julianna of when she'd texted out a picture of Sandra and Blair so that his mom, the principal, would find out about their secret relationship. Julianna hadn't been the only one who didn't approve of their dating. She could now admit that it had been a horrible thing to do. The guilt had settled heavily over her for months. Just another thing she'd been trying to escape that had followed her.

"What are you saying? That I should try to hook up with her?" Scott had stopped walking and was now giving her the most intense stare she had ever received. It made her pulse spike, and she knew they needed to keep walking or she'd end up kissing him instead. Which was absolutely not something she could do. Ever.

Julianna released a heavy sigh and pulled on Scott's arm to get him to keep walking. She liked this. Holding a boy's hand. Why did it feel so intimate, like it meant more than if she *had* kissed him? "No, I'm not. It's just..." She gave a quick shake of her head. "You asked why I came here. And believe it or not, you were right. It wasn't to learn to use a lasso. It was to escape home. My town. And the people in it. Miraculously, though, the two people I needed to escape the most managed to follow me here."

"Sounds like they have a purpose in being here, just as much as you do."

She threw him a side glance. "What, like we were all destined to come here at the same time—like, fate?"

Scott shrugged. "I just think there is purpose in everything.

And if you are all here, despite your best efforts to get away from them, maybe there is something you need to work out. And I don't think it involves me breaking them up."

Julianna didn't believe in God or purpose or fate or destiny. She didn't believe that the universe arranged everything for a reason. Because her life never went the way she wanted it to—needed it to. Even now, fate was laughing at her. Mocking her. Telling her, *Better luck next time.*

"I was in love with him for three years," she said after a few minutes of silence. "Even was assigned to a school project together. I thought that was fate. It wasn't. Unless you consider it fate that we would work together at the library, and that was where he met Sandra. And then I had to pretty much do the entire project on my own because he was too busy drooling over her to think straight."

"Unrequited love. That's the worst."

Julianna had to stop herself from rolling her eyes. Maybe he was trying to be nice—show some empathy—but it only managed to make her feel worse. "You wouldn't know anything about that." She couldn't imagine anyone not being in love with the famous Scott Dallenforth. He could get any girl he wanted.

"Sure I do. I'm looking at her." And then he grinned in a way that said he was totally messing with her.

And it was in the worst way possible.

7

SCOTT

Scott started when Jules turned a look of death on him. And he thought he'd rather die than be on the receiving end of that again. She dropped his hand and marched forward, half-falling as she did.

He called after her. "What? I'm just trying to lighten the mood. Seriously, you've been giving me the cold shoulder ever since we met. I feel like I'm doing all the work in this relationship."

Jules turned back, and it was no longer a look of death. More like Medusa. Scott felt his blood turn to stone—he couldn't move.

"Maybe this is hard for someone like you to understand," she said, "because you have no scarcity of girls or dates or people falling at your feet, but it's not so easy for the rest of us. Or maybe it's just me, because sometimes it feels like that. But you don't know what it's like to have someone you'd do anything for ignore you...treat you like you don't exist. It's horrible." She paused, her gaze dropping. "I know Blair's favorite color, his hobbies, what foods he's allergic to. I know that he keeps his hair long enough so that when he's frustrated, he can rake his fingers through it. The barber cut it too short one time, and he was on edge for three weeks until it grew long enough. I don't know if Sandra even knows all of that."

Scott wanted to say, *Because she's not a stalker*. But now didn't seem the right time for it. And the fact was that Jules had a point. He had no idea what that was like. "You're right. I shouldn't have joked about something I have no experience in. But I do know what it's like to never be able to seriously date anyone. I always assume every girl I go out with is after my money or my fame, or more likely both. It's the reason I quit going to school. My mom thinks I have no direction and that I'm going to regret not getting a better education. And she's not completely off base. But really, it was because I was tired of going to a normal school when I'm *not* normal. It sounds conceited, but it was impossible for me to have a typical high school experience. And it will be impossible for me to have a typical college experience. You've seen what the past day has been like for me here. Everyone either smothers me or avoids me like the plague. And I'm over it. So I might as well live up this life while I got it, right? At least when I hang out with other celebrities, everyone is famous, so no one cares who you are. That's what has had to become my new normal."

Scott fell silent, his breaths heavy. Admitting all that had taken more than he'd expected. And to someone who was practically a stranger, no less.

"I guess the saying about the grass always being greener is true, huh?" Julianna asked, making her way back to him and taking his hand.

"Your situation still sucks worse," he said as they began walking again. "Maybe there is a way I can help."

"What did you have in mind?" Jules's lips quirked up, and excitement had ignited behind her eyes.

"There's a swimming party tonight. Let's go together. I'll

make sure that Blair will be so jealous, he can't stop staring. Not to mention everyone else in the place."

The excitement died, and Jules's lips pursed. Was that not the right thing to say? He was sure that she looked hot in a bikini. All he had to do was throw out some compliments, maybe a kiss on the cheek, and bada bing bada boom, everyone in the place is jealous of the girl who says no one sees her. What was the problem?

"Like I said. You don't understand." Jules didn't let go of his hand, still helping support him as they finished the last two hours of the hike. But she didn't say anything more either. That kind of silence made the two hours seem like twelve. He tried to say sorry, but he didn't know what he was apologizing for, and so it fell on deaf ears.

Maybe he had lost touch with reality.

Or maybe he'd never had it in the first place.

SCOTT'S GAZE kept flitting to the second floor of the barn. He knew Jules was up there somewhere, training to be a counselor in the kids' camp. He wished the ranch allowed guys to do it. Scott would be perfect as a counselor. He loved kids—they were freakin' hilarious—and they loved him back because he let them use him as a human jungle gym. It was the perfect partnership. He wondered how Jules was going to fare. She didn't seem like the human jungle gym type. Also, he had overheard that goth girl, Sandra, talking at breakfast. Turned out she was also a counselor in the kids' camp.

"You listening, Dallenforth?"

Everyone's attention turned to Scott, who didn't have the slightest idea what was happening.

"Sure am."

"What was the last thing I said?" Jimmy must be a parent because that was something his mother would say.

Scott glanced around, hoping someone would give him a clue. Penny, who it turned out was one of the activity guides, made some sort of motion with her hands, like she was raising a flag. "We're going to be...practicing...raising the..." Penny gave a slight shake of her head. "Pledge of..." Another shake. "Roping steer."

Everyone laughed, and Penny groaned.

"Nice try, rock star." Did Jimmy really need to bring any more attention to the fact? Couldn't he just be Scott from Southern California for a while? "We're going to be learning to belay each other on the rock wall." He nodded to the wall behind them that stretched up past the second floor of the barn. "And then after lunch, I'll be taking you out on the four-wheelers to give you an idea what the trails are like. After this week, you'll be on your own, so I suggest you pay attention." He shot Scott a warning glance.

Scott rolled his eyes. "Yeah, yeah. I got it. Pay attention."

This was not helping with his popularity—or lack thereof. And neither was the ridiculous getup he was wearing. The hat he was required to wear looked like something his dad would wear hiking, and the khaki shirt actually had a collar and a front pocket. Who went four-wheeling in this kind of getup?

No one.

And yet, here he was.

Scott wondered if it was too late to call up his chauffeur and escape the type of hell that only his parents could come up with. He probably would have, too, if Penny hadn't walked up to him.

"How did you get roping steer from this?" She repeated the motion she'd done earlier.

"I don't know. How do you get rock climbing from it?"

Penny did the motion again. "I'm pulling the rope tight as you climb. I'm belaying."

Scott threw his hands into the air. "How was I supposed to know that? I've never rock climbed before."

"Neither have I, but I watch TV."

"I don't have time for that. I'm a busy guy."

Penny laughed. "And to think that everyone gets nervous around you. All they have to do is talk to you and they'd be put right at ease."

He wasn't able to come up with a sarcastic comeback before Jimmy called him out in front of the group. Again. "Rock star, you planning on wearing a harness, or you going to free climb?"

Scott glanced around and noticed that everyone else was already tightening their harnesses, and they seemed all too pleased that he had messed up. What was it about him that made them so happy to see him fail? He didn't try to act better than anyone else, and yet it was like they had already decided that he thought exactly that.

"I'll take a harness." Before he thought better of it, he added, "Penny needs one too."

"Way to throw me under the bus," she muttered as Jimmy held out two harnesses.

"A little quicker next time," Jimmy said to Penny, but that was it. No taunts. No teasing.

And yet Scott was the one everyone was jealous of.

It didn't take long to figure out who the climbers were and who was lucky that, as guides, they could keep their feet on the ground.

Turned out that Scott wasn't so bad, and he made it up to the top quicker than anyone else. After he'd pulled the rope to the bell at the top of the wall, he wished he'd slowed down a bit, or maybe not made it to the top at all. As much as he didn't like when people took pictures of him when he failed at things or made a fool of himself, it was better than the looks and murmurings he was getting now. The girls, acting like he was God's gift to rock climbing, and the guys, looking at him like he was trying to show off. Trying to show that there wasn't anything he couldn't do.

It didn't matter what Scott did. He couldn't win.

Except with one person.

Jimmy strode up to Scott, and for once actually seemed pleased. "Scott, since you seem to have experience with this, why don't you belay Penny?" He turned to the rest of the group. "This is what you'll be doing for our guests."

"Oh, I've never actually belayed anyone before."

"It's easy. You'll have no problem with it."

And then Jimmy showed Scott how to hold the rope and how to use his own body weight, and gave tips for controlling Penny's descent.

"No offense," Penny whispered as she clicked a helmet into place, "but I'd feel more comfortable with Jimmy at the ropes." Her curly hair shot out in all directions from under the helmet, accenting her wide eyes.

Scott could admit that he was a bit nervous at the prospect of doing this by himself with everyone watching. But the way Jimmy had explained things to him, it didn't seem difficult. And their fearless leader was there if anything went wrong.

Scott's gaze swept upwards over the rock wall. It didn't look as high from the bottom. After he'd rung the bell at the top, he'd made the mistake of looking down, and everything had started spinning. Good thing all he'd had to do at that point was push off and rappel down. No skill needed.

Movement on the second floor caught Scott's attention and he turned. Leaning over the balcony, watching, was Jules. The goth chick that she'd been trying to avoid stood next to her, alongside one other girl he hadn't met. And they seemed to be waiting for him to belay Penny. Everyone wanted a piece of the action.

Scott's attention turned back to the rock wall. Several people stood to the side and had their phones out. Probably hoping there would be something worth catching that would boost their social media accounts. He was pretty sure the ranch had signed something saying he couldn't do pictures or autographs, the whole "respecting his privacy" thing, but no one seemed to care about enforcing it. And honestly, things might get worse if they did. Then people would be trying to sneak pictures rather than doing it out in the open. Scott preferred to know what kind of pictures to expect to pop up all over the internet rather than be blindsided.

"You ready for this?" he asked Penny.

Penny was one of the last few who hadn't climbed the wall yet, and he thought that might have been on purpose. Her face was three shades paler, and she looked like she might puke.

When she didn't answer, he said, "We don't have to do this."

She gave a quick shake of her head, and her mouth tightened into a determined line. "Yes, I do. This is my job. If I don't do it, then what's going to happen when someone needs help?"

Penny gave a quick tug on the rope that was attached to her harness, then placed a foot on the first rock. It was another moment before she pushed herself up onto it, and Scott could see her whole frame shaking.

"You can do it, Penny," someone shouted from the second floor. Jules.

It seemed to give Penny courage, and she pushed up to the next rock. Jules whistled, which got Penny up to the next one. And then Jules started chanting Penny's name. And Penny kept going. Then others joined in, and soon the whole barn rang with Penny's name as she moved from rock to rock.

Scott made sure he kept the rope tight just in case anything happened, but he was no longer worried for the curly haired girl. Because even though Jules didn't think of herself as someone who made friends easily, it was clear to Scott that Jules was one of the best people out there to have as a friend.

And he was sure that because of her support, Penny, who had struggled making it to the second rock, was now going to make it to the very top. At least, until Penny made the mistake of looking down before she got there. She was about three-fourths of the way up, and Scott knew the moment that Penny wasn't going to go any further. The shaking returned, and she flattened herself against the wall, clinging to it as if her life depended on it. She probably thought it did.

"Bring me down, Scott," she said, her voice shaking as much as the rest of her.

Scott leaned back, prepared to use his body weight as Jimmy had instructed. "I'm ready for you, but you have to let go of the wall."

A pause.

"I can't."

Jimmy walked up and stood by Scott's side. "This is good practice for you," he mumbled. "You're going to have a lot of folks who are pressured to climb by their parents or their boyfriend or whoever, and you have to talk them down. Nice calm voice."

"Did you know coming down is the most fun part of it all?" Scott asked Penny, tightening his grip on the rope. "How often do you get to feel like you're flying? Soaring midair, nothing but you and the—"

"Not helping, Scott," Penny called down.

Okay, new tactic.

"Close your eyes and imagine you're on the beach." Scott used the soft voice that his mom's meditation video used. "You hear the waves crashing against the shore. A seagull cries off in the distance."

"Seriously?" Now Penny sounded mad. Which was the opposite of what his mom's videos did. She was usually half asleep by the end of them. Sometimes all the way asleep.

Penny turned her gaze on Scott, her eyebrows furrowed.

Scott swallowed hard. He'd never seen her anything but happy, and this new angry Penny made him nervous. He had a feeling that he'd need to keep her out of arm's reach for a while.

"It's called meditation, Penny."

"It's called lame."

Luckily Penny slipped from the rock she was holding, and she screamed as she swung away from the wall. Jimmy stepped forward, ready to grab the rope if need be, but Scott had her. He slowly lowered her as Jimmy had taught him, but then stopped a foot off the ground.

"What are you doing?" she yelled, panic lacing her tone.

Jimmy threw him a curious look. "Yes, what are you doing?"

"Apologize," Scott said.

Penny flapped her arms and legs wildly, like that would help her close the rest of the distance. "What?"

"I was just trying to help, and you yelled at me. I would like an apology, please. And a promise that you aren't going to murder me once you're on the ground."

Penny turned a death glare on Scott. She must have learned it from Jules. "Or what? You going to keep me up here all day?"

"Maybe."

Not really. But Scott had expected Penny to immediately soften, maybe even laugh about it and apologize, and then they'd act like it had been one big joke.

That wasn't happening. And if anything, Penny was getting madder.

"I think you better let her down, Scott," Jimmy said, his voice quiet.

"Yeah, okay."

Scott lowered her the last foot, but as soon as she touched down, he let go of the rope and walked away. It didn't matter. The whole thing had been recorded on people's phones anyway. As soon as they got somewhere with cell service, everything would be uploaded. One final shot of him walking away wouldn't make a difference.

"Hey, wait up." Scott heard Penny calling him, but he kept walking.

It had been childish, keeping her in the air like that, demanding an apology. This was the type of thing that wasn't good for his public image—that he felt entitled to always get what he wanted, even if it meant stringing up girls who were terrified of heights.

Way to go, Scott.

"Fine," she called after him. "But I thought you should know that I just quit."

8

JULIANNA

As soon as Julianna saw Scott leave, then Penny in tears, she knew her own job training could wait. She rushed down the steps that would lead her out of the barn, ignoring Sandra's calls of "Where are you going?"

By the time she made it outside, it looked like Scott and Penny were going to have a standoff. Both had their hands on their hips, only missing the guns and holsters.

"That's ridiculous," Scott was saying. "Just because you got a little freaked out up there—"

"I was more than a little freaked out," Penny said. "Everyone thinks because I try to be happy and find the best in everything that I don't get scared or mad or wish I could murder a rock star. I feel everything, I just don't usually show it."

"There's nothing wrong with not being happy all the time, and there's nothing wrong with being scared. Besides, you don't even have to climb the wall with the guests."

"You think four-wheeling or the zipline is going to go any better? I can't do this."

Scott raised an eyebrow and put on his serious face. "Yes, you can. I saw the way you moved up the wall. You just need time to gain confidence." When Penny didn't respond, Scott said, "You need me to hang you midair again until you start believing me? I'll do it."

Penny folded her arms over her chest and scowled. "Not helping. Per your usual."

"Hey, hey, hey." Julianna jumped in between the two before anything else could be said that they'd regret later. She placed a hand on Penny's shoulder. "Let's walk this off and reconvene in an hour, yeah?"

"That will be kind of difficult when she won't be here in an hour," Scott said.

Julianna whipped toward Penny. "What is he talking about?"

When Penny's gaze dropped to the ground and she didn't answer, Scott did it for her.

"She quit."

Julianna studied Penny. She looked nothing like the girl Julianna had come to know over the past few days. Quiet. Withdrawn. "That can't be true." Julianna's words were for Scott, but her gaze didn't leave Penny. "She would never quit. It's not in her nature."

"How would you know?" Penny asked, her gaze snapping up and meeting Julianna's. "You don't know me."

"I know that you are—"

"You know what I want you to see," Penny interrupted. She paused, a guilty look flashing across her face, and she sucked in a long breath. "When they said I would be an activity guide, I didn't know what that meant. I didn't realize I'd need to do all of the activities myself. I don't mind belaying. I don't mind teaching people gun safety or helping guide hikes. But I'm freaked out by almost everything we're doing here. Heights included. The only way I made it here on the airplane was by sitting in the very middle where I couldn't see out the window. And I... I just can't do it."

Moisture welled up in Penny's eyes, and Julianna didn't know how to respond. What did you say to someone who appeared to have more confidence than you'd ever known, and then you find out they are just as fragile and broken as you are? She looked to Scott for help, but he seemed to be just as lost as she was.

"I'm sorry. For not bringing you down right away," he finally said.

Penny's lips turned up, and a flicker of the girl Julianna had first met returned. "You were right. You were trying to help, and I was freaking out on you. All I had to do was let go. It's me who is sorry. And I promise not to murder you."

Scott snorted. "Thanks."

"Oh, and for the record, it did feel a little like flying." Penny was at least smiling now. She pulled in a shuddered breath and placed her hands on her hips. "I know I was only here a few days, but I'm going to miss this place." She turned toward the field, her gaze taking in the area, as if she were already saying goodbye.

"No," Julianna said, the word bursting from her lips. "No. You are not quitting."

Penny seemed to have gotten out whatever emotions had needed to escape, and she turned back to Julianna with a sad smile. "I can't be what they need me to be."

Jimmy burst out of the barn just then. His gaze settled on them, and he hurried over. "You are not quitting."

"That's what I said," Julianna said, shooting Penny a triumphant smile.

"But I—"

Jimmy held up a hand. "I can put you on duties that don't involve rock climbing."

"But it's not going to be just that. I'm scared of most of the stuff you provide for your guests. I thought I could handle it. I thought it wouldn't be a big deal, that I was just assisting. And I saw it as an opportunity to do better—be better. Overcome things. But I was wrong."

Penny was getting that sad look again. But this time it was accompanied by something worse. Desperation. And it appeared to be desperation to get out—to get as far as she could from the ranch and her place in it.

"Have her trade with me," Julianna said abruptly. She didn't know where the idea came from, but as soon as she said it, it made sense. Penny would be able to stay, and Julianna wouldn't have to work with Sandra. The past two hours had been torture. Sandra was nice enough—almost too nice—but that was the problem. Julianna didn't want to like her. And Sandra was trying to become friends. Julianna knew her feelings for Blair weren't Sandra's fault. But it still hurt. "I'll be an activity guide. I've never done most of it, but I can learn. Penny can do kids' camp."

Penny's lips parted in surprise, and her gaze whipped to Jimmy. "Is that possible? Could I do that?"

Jimmy was silent for a moment, taking in the three of them. "I have to make sure Kassandra is okay with it, but I don't see why not. Although I still think we can work something out for you, Penny, to be an activity gui—"

"I'll do the camp," she said quickly, and then a grin broke out across her face. "I'll absolutely do it. I love kids. I think. I'm an only child. But I'm sure I'll love kids more than rock climbing."

Jimmy laughed. "Well, you are going to get a really quick lesson in kids, because our first guests arrive in ten days."

"As long as they don't string me up on the rock-climbing rope, I think I'm going to be just fine." She shot a smirk in Scott's direction.

Penny was back.

Scott threw out his arms and gave an exasperated sigh. "I. Was. Trying. To. Help."

Penny smiled. "I know." And then she ran toward the barn and called over her shoulder, "I'll tell the goth girl about the change of plans."

Jimmy gave a rare smile and then extended an arm toward the barn. "Shall we? I guess we need to train you how to put on a harness properly and see if you can get up the rock wall."

Julianna's stomach suddenly felt queasy, but she shoved it down. She had chosen this, and from the look Scott was giving her, she could tell he wasn't disappointed by the change of events. In fact, he seemed quite happy about it. Which made her wonder if the queasiness had to do with the rock wall or the fact that she was going to be able to work with Scott every day for the rest of the summer.

Blair. She had meant Blair.

Because really, Scott was ridiculous and self-centered and... She stopped herself. That had been the old him—the one who had arrived in his cowboy hat. Or so she had thought. Now, she wasn't so sure who the real Scott Dallenforth was.

"As long as you don't have Scott belaying me. I saw how the last one went down," she told Jimmy, moving toward the barn.

"Hey," Scott protested, following her. "I was in complete control."

Julianna threw a grin over her shoulder. "That's what worries me."

IT TURNED out that Julianna hadn't needed to worry how she'd do as an activity guide. She could clean a gun just as well as any of the guys, she could rappel faster, and she could get the hook out of a fish and toss the fish back into the stocked pond cleaner and quicker.

"Guests start arriving tomorrow," Scott said, walking up beside her, paintball coveralls hanging over one arm. "Going out four-wheeling with your friends is one thing. Being responsible for strangers not dying is a completely different animal."

Julianna threw him an amused smile as she balanced on one leg and slipped her other leg into her coveralls. "You trying to get into my head, Dallenforth?"

"No, no, just trying to prepare you for things to come." He returned her smile as he began to get his own coveralls on.

"What I think is that you're scared."

Scott's mouth dropped open in mock offense. "How could you say such a thing? I'm the best thing out there since... anything." His gaze whipped around like he wanted to make sure no one else had heard that, then he dropped his voice to a whisper. "I don't really think that, you know. Even if everyone else thinks I do."

Julianna studied him as she zipped up her coveralls. They were probably three sizes too big, but she'd been one of the last to get hers. "I know." She looked down and shook her legs. The excess material bounced up and down. "Think I could win any beauty pageants in this thing?"

He looked her up and down. "Absolutely. Stunning."

She felt heat rushing into her cheeks, and she tried to cover it up with a laugh. "Really. Coveralls do it for you, huh?"

"If you're the one wearing them." As soon as the words left Scott's lips, he froze, as did Julianna.

There he went again, falling into old habits, acting like Scott Dallenforth, the rock star. She'd made it very clear to him that he was not to flirt with her—that his usual tactics didn't work on girls like her. Nor did she want him to try. It was apparently too much effort for him to restrain himself, because casual flirtation was what Scott Dallenforth did best.

And it was the type of thing that broke the hearts of girls like Julianna.

"I didn't mean..." Scott didn't seem to know how to finish that sentence.

"I know," Julianna said, her words coming out much too quickly. She picked up a paintball gun from the activity counter in an attempt to cover up how flustered Scott made her. "I've never been paintballing. Shooting things never seemed like the type of thing I'd enjoy. Making those clay pigeons explode last week was strangely satisfying, though. I'm thinking this could be fun."

Scott eyed her warily. "Yes, it is. And I'm starting to think it will be a good thing if we are on the same team."

"Gather up," Jimmy yelled, and everyone in their blue striped coveralls approached the front of the barn. "The instructions I give you today are going to be the same instructions you will need to give the guests, so pay attention."

Julianna tried to catch everything, but she was distracted by Scott, who seemed unable to stop watching her. When she'd meet his gaze, his attention would return to Jimmy, but it didn't take long for his focus to meander back to her.

"Pay attention," she whispered, her gaze remaining on Jimmy.

"I am."

"To the instructions."

"I am."

"Then why do you keep looking at me?"

"Because you're a better view."

Julianna's gaze shot back to Scott. He smiled, then turned back to Jimmy.

Okay, she could write off the first compliment as an off-hand remark. One that he'd already started apologizing for. But this—this was completely different and deliberate.

And Julianna didn't know if she liked that or not.

"I really need to stop wearing coveralls," she muttered.

9

SCOTT

Scott followed the group out across the field. He'd thought that might be where they'd play, but Jimmy kept walking up a small hill just beyond. Jules was walking near the front, her pace brisk, like she was purposely keeping distance between them.

He hadn't meant to say what he had, that he enjoyed looking at Jules more than Jimmy (which should have been a no-brainer), but Scott doubted that Jules would be comforted by that fact. In his experience, girls tended to like being flirted with on purpose.

Scott hadn't been able to help it, though. Jules had looked adorable in those coveralls that all but drowned her, with the paintball mask sitting on top of her head. That, coupled with her holding her paintball gun like she was Rambo, was enough for anyone to stop and stare. Not in a you-look-ridiculous kind of way. But in an I-don't-know-why-I-find-this-attractive-but-I-kind-of-want-to-kiss-you kind of way.

And maybe Jules had seen all that in the way he'd looked at her. And maybe she had every right to be keeping her distance.

Except, walking at the back of the group, alone—Scott

missed her. Ever since coming to the ranch, he was used to falling behind, wanting the least confrontation possible. But he had gotten used to Jules being back there with him—staying behind so he wouldn't have to be alone.

Scott needed a friend, not a date. And he had confused those two things for a brief moment. But he wouldn't make that mistake again. Jules was someone he needed for more than just a good night on the town, and he needed to make things right with her.

Scott was so lost in his thoughts, he made it to the top of the hill before he realized he'd even been climbing one. And he knew immediately that they'd arrived. A clearing stretched before them, but it wasn't empty. It was littered with old tires, a broken-down car, a smattering of trees, and remnants of old paint from previous wars. To the right of them sat a wooden structure that looked like it had once been a shed. Except the back had been cut off, so it was half a shed with a window facing the field and a ledge that extended from the open side of the building out over the dirt and sagebrush.

"This is where I will be watching the game," Jimmy said, patting the side of the shed. "When you hear the whistle, the game is over. No more shots. Got it?"

A murmur of agreement rippled through the crowd.

"I'm handing out strips of fabric. Tie it around one arm over your bicep so we know which team you're on. Blue, you're starting behind the tree line on the right. Red, you're starting behind the tree line on the left."

Scott tried to get a look at which color Jules had received, but she turned to the side as another girl helped her tie the strip of fabric. It wasn't until after Jimmy had given Scott a red strip that he saw Jules had blue. He tried to trade with the kid next to him, but the boy just raised an eyebrow and then tied his strip around his own arm.

It wasn't that being on the opposite team from Jules made Scott nervous. He had gone paintballing with his friends dozens of times and knew she had never been. But he'd gotten used to Jules being on his team—having his back. And it felt wrong for it to be any other way. Not to mention that she seemed to have grown an affinity for guns over the past week.

"Looks like we're on the same team, rock star," someone said.

Scott turned and found himself facing Blair. The guy that Jules talked nonstop about, while at the same time getting mad at Scott if he ever brought the guy up in conversation. The guy that Jules was in love with.

Scott shoved down the feelings of annoyance at Blair for hurting Jules. He knew more than anyone that you couldn't help who you fell for, and who fell for you. Scott couldn't date every girl who ever showed interest, including those who claimed they wanted to marry him. Especially those ones.

But Blair didn't know what was standing right in front of him —what an amazing girl he could have. And how she had just been waiting for him to notice her. Jealousy reared up, and Scott attempted to shove that down too.

"Yeah, looks like it," Scott said, offering Blair a friendly smile. He hoped it didn't look too forced.

"You any good with this thing?" Blair held up his own gun.

Scott puffed out his chest a little, not that it did much in those big coveralls. He'd be lucky to get through a whole game without tripping over the fabric that nearly covered his toes. "I've been known to win." He lifted a shoulder, like winning paintball games was a daily occurrence.

Blair grinned. "Good. Because see that guy over there?" He pointed to a tall guy with blonde hair and thick arms. "That's my best friend, Cameron. And we have to take him out first. Once he's gone, the rest will be easy."

This was it. Scott's chance to get in good with one of the

guys. Even if it meant teaming up with Blair, he'd take whatever chance he could get.

Blair had been kind of standoffish from the beginning, along with his friend that they apparently needed to add to the top of their hit list. Scott had heard that their girlfriends had freaked out when they'd discovered that Scott was working at the ranch. It had been the normal type of fangirl freak-out, but it still hadn't settled well with the guys.

If Blair saw what a good guy Scott was, if he warmed up, then maybe the rest of the guys would thaw out a bit too.

"Sure, no problem. You thinking of flanking him, or more of a distraction kind of situation?" Scott asked, flashing another smile Blair's way. He realized that might be a bit much and dialed it back so it was more a look of amusement.

It seemed to work because Blair studied him for a moment, seeming surprised. "Guess you're not just a pretty face behind a microphone, huh?"

"I try really hard not to be." As soon as Scott said it, he wished he could take it back. His words had sounded desperate, like he was trying too hard. Because he was. But he didn't want Blair knowing it.

It didn't seem to faze Blair, though. Instead, when he noticed Cameron watching them, smirking, he lowered his voice to a conspiratorial whisper and gave Scott instructions.

It seemed a bit primitive, but Scott thought it could work. It took all your basic paintball tactics and rolled them into one. Go around the side, work in pairs, use the trees as cover, move quickly, and then ambush. No sweat.

As Jimmy stood up front and gave the instructions that they'd need to give to the guests, Scott tried not to think about the possibility of having to shoot Jules. And he continued not thinking about it as they marched toward their starting positions.

"You know what to do," Blair whispered, and then disappeared to the left through the trees.

Okay. Scott could do this. And along the way to taking down Cameron, he would impress his team by taking out all the others too, sniper-style. Jules included. Scott paused. Taking out the other team single-handedly wouldn't win him any friends. In fact, it would probably have the opposite effect. But hiding out or dying too quickly would do the same.

It was a lose-lose situation, like usual.

Scott frowned, then decided the only thing he should do was help take out Blair's friend. He'd already been enlisted for that task, and if he managed to succeed, leaving the way open for his team to take out the rest, that might just do it.

And he wouldn't have to shoot Jules in the process.

Win-win-win.

Scott lowered his mask, tightened his grip on his gun, and moved to the right. No movement through the trees up ahead.

A crack. Leaves rustling.

He slipped behind a bush and saw a member of the other team. Was that his target? He couldn't tell with the mask on. Everyone looked the same. The person didn't look tall enough to be Cameron, though, so Scott continued on.

The first shot was fired. Someone walked out, hands above their head, their gun held high in the sky. A member of his team was the first casualty.

No one was daring run into the middle of the clearing yet. The broken-down car looked eerie, just sitting there. Waiting.

Scott saw a flash of blue stripes. Did he dare shoot and give away his position, or should he stay focused on Cameron?

Another shot. Another casualty from his own team.

Where were his other team members? Were they just hiding, waiting for this to all be over?

Scott realized he was doing the exact same thing, hesitating, not doing anything useful. It was after another member of his team was shot that Scott decided he needed to just take these guys out, because it was apparent no one else was going to do it.

Except, everyone seemed to have disappeared. He walked and walked—and saw no one.

That was when a lone figure walked into the middle of the clearing. No paint on them. They were still in the game. But they were just walking out like they didn't have a care in the world. And it was one of Scott's teammates. This was getting ridiculous, and Scott was starting to think they were doing it on purpose. Like they wanted him to fail and were willing to sacrifice themselves for it.

"Hey, Cameron. I challenge you to a duel!"

It was Blair. What was he doing? This had not been part of the plan. They were supposed to come from opposite directions so they could trap Cameron in the middle. Of course, that would have relied on Scott actually having some way of knowing where the others were located. He wasn't used to playing in a field this large.

"Nice distraction, but I'm not falling for it," Cameron yelled back.

Oh, brilliant. Blair was using one of the oldest tricks in the book. Distraction. And at the same time, he was letting Scott know where Cameron was. Scott moved quickly now, not worrying as much about the noise he was making.

Closing in.

He could see Cameron just ahead, inside the tree line. Except he wasn't alone. There were four members of the blue team, all standing with their backs to each other, so they formed a sort of diamond.

That was why they'd been able to take everyone out. There would be no sneaking up on them, not to mention that Scott had no idea which one was Cameron. He'd have to try to shoot them all before they got him.

A crack of a branch from Scott's other side. One of his teammates. Scott gave a quick shake of his head, and they paused.

The blue team's attention was all on Blair, who was walking slowly toward them, not even using the car for cover. Scott thought the guy should at least use one of the monster truck tires, but Blair didn't bother.

A member of the blue diamond raised their gun to shoot Blair. "I'm sorry it had to end like this, friend."

Cameron.

Scott whipped his gun up and fired. Red paint splattered Cameron just under his armpit. The other three whipped toward him, and Scott saw no way out. He'd just have to shoot as many as he could before they realized what was happening. It turned out that Scott only needed to shoot one of them, his teammate managing to take out the other two. Except the diamond had been a distraction of its own.

Four more members of the blue team seemed to materialize from nowhere. One aimed their gun at Blair, whose attention was elsewhere.

"Watch out," Scott yelled, then jumped in front of the gunman and shot. Blair spun around, but it was too late for him to do anything. Red exploded over the other guy's heart just as blue exploded over the same spot on Scott's chest.

Ow.

For a moment, Scott wondered if the other guy had even felt it, his coveralls were so baggy.

Oh, shoot.

Baggy coveralls.

He had just shot Jules.

10

JULIANNA

O uch.

Julianna hadn't ever played paintball before. She hadn't realized how much it would hurt and hadn't even considered being shot in the chest. And right in the most sensitive spot, no less. Her first instinct was to grab it, cradle it. Maybe whimper a little.

Yeah, that wasn't going to happen. Especially considering who had just shot her.

Scott Dallenforth.

It was such a relief, she couldn't stop herself from smiling. Julianna had been so worried when he'd complimented her— flirted—that she was just another girl to Scott. But now that she knew that when it came down to it, he would shoot her, Julianna realized she had nothing to worry about. Scott wasn't trying to get her to kiss him— to add her to his wall of trophies. Because shooting a girl was certainly not the way to her heart.

So, why did she feel more attracted to Scott now than she had an hour ago?

Why did she kind of wish he would kiss her?

Julianna shook her head. That was the pain talking.

Scott seemed frozen in place, like he was unsure how she was going to react. But there was still a war going on, and she didn't want to be in the middle of it, so she motioned with her head for him to follow and then held her gun over her head as she walked past the broken-down car and a few Julianna-sized tires, and back up the hill to the shed.

"Very impressive out there," Jimmy said, giving them each a nod. And he really did seem impressed. "Just two left on each side now. Things should get interesting."

Julianna took her mask off and shook out her hair. There was paint in it. She grinned, excited that she had something to show for her first paintball game. Other than a bruise that she most definitely was not going to be able to show off. She threw a glance at Scott, who was just taking his mask off. He met her gaze, his eyes troubled.

"What's wrong? You just took out like five guys. I'd think you'd be happier," she said, her lips lifting at one corner. Gosh, he was good-looking. Julianna didn't usually allow herself to look too long, afraid what that might do to her.

She had had reason to be scared.

Julianna glanced away, begging her heart rate to slow. Forcing herself to see Scott as a friend. Not as someone who could make her breathing stall.

Scott didn't answer her, and she didn't push him any further. They watched as Blair took out the last two members of Julianna's team in a good old-fashioned showdown.

It was painful to watch, but not as painful as the silence that had settled between her and Scott.

Jimmy blew his whistle, indicating the game was over. Once Blair and the others rejoined them, Jimmy declared the red team the winners. The team cheered, but it was nothing compared to the cheering that came from everyone when they discovered they had two hours off to eat and clean up.

Everyone filed out of the back of the shed, and Julianna moved to follow them. Except, Scott didn't. Even though his entire team was grinning and clapping him on the back, telling him he did amazing—even Blair—Scott didn't seem as excited as everyone else. Sure, he smiled and said thanks, but his smile disappeared as soon as they looked away. And then he sat on the edge of the shed and watched the others pushing each other down the hill as they headed back to the barn.

Julianna sat down next to him. The ledge was high enough that her feet didn't quite touch the ground and they swung over the dirt.

"It's beautiful up here," she said, taking in the view. From the top of the hill, she could see the stables to their left and guest cabins to their right. The barn and lodge sat in the middle with a fishing pond just beyond. When Scott stayed silent, she tried again. "Looks like you've won over your bunkmates. Funny the things that will make someone a friend. Like being really good at shooting people."

"I'm sorry," Scott said, the words fast and explosive. "For shooting you. If I would have known it was you—" He must have seen Julianna's stricken expression, because his words faltered.

"Please..." Julianna said, her voice quiet. "Please don't say that."

Scott hesitated, seemingly unsure how to proceed. "You don't want me to apologize?"

"No. I don't," Julianna's words came out angrier than she had intended. But she didn't want to be just like all the other girls—didn't want him to treat her like them. "I don't see you apologizing to anyone else you shot."

Scott raised a shoulder. "They're guys. And you're...you."

Julianna pushed off from the ledge and landed in the dirt behind the paintball shed. "Because I'm a girl. And because if you say nice things and then spare me in a paintball game, you think I'll fall for you, like every other girl." Her voice quieted. "And then I become invisible again. Like every other girl."

Scott's lips parted in surprise. "Is that why you thought I was apologizing? Because I was trying to start something with you? I just felt bad because I shot you in a place where I'm pretty sure it hurt. A lot."

"Oh." Julianna's breath caught, and it felt like her heart had landed in her shoes. Scott Dallenforth had no feelings for her. No attraction. Which was what she had said she wanted. Multiple times. It should be a relief.

But she'd been lying to him. To herself. Anything other than admitting the truth.

Julianna had finally gotten over Blair. By falling for someone who was so much more out of her league, they weren't even playing the same sport. "I...better go. Need to shower and eat and all that."

Scott jumped down from the shed and landed next to her. "Hey, I didn't mean—"

"It's fine," Julianna said, holding up a hand, stopping him. "I have paint in my hair and..." Her words trailed off as Scott reached forward and lifted the lock of hair where the green paint was already drying.

"I think you should keep it like this."

The way Scott was looking at her—Julianna felt her walls crumbling, and panic rose in her chest. "I—"

And then Julianna did the unthinkable.

She kissed Scott Dallenforth. More like threw herself at him. The kiss was so short, she didn't even know if he had kissed her back.

And then she ran away, tripping over those stupid coveralls all the way to the barn.

11

SCOTT

Scott leaned against the rec desk and threw a glance toward Jules, who was belaying someone on the rock wall. Two days had passed since she'd kissed Scott. Two days that she had been avoiding him, and he hadn't exactly gone out of his way to remedy that. It wasn't that he didn't want to talk to her. He just had no idea what he'd say when he finally found his voice.

Scott had relived the moment at the paintball field a hundred times since she'd kissed him. He was used to girls making the first move—but not the way Julianna had. Like she hadn't wanted to. Evidenced by the fact that she had then run away.

If he were being honest with himself, he'd admit that if Jules hadn't kissed him at that moment, he would have done it first. She was unlike anyone he'd ever met. She didn't care who he was. If anything, the fact that he was Scott Dallenforth was a strike against him.

And he liked that. He could be himself around her—could be human. In return, she was beautiful and funny and compassionate. What more could he ask for?

"Oy, rock star," Jimmy called, breaking into Scott's thoughts. "Your turn." The nickname now held affection, as opposed to the hint of mockery Scott had detected when he'd first arrived.

Scott pushed away from the desk, tearing his gaze from Jules. "Coming." He'd been doing nothing but practicing cleaning guns in the back room that day. He could understand why it was so important for them to be comfortable with the task. Unfortunately, it also gave his mind ample time to wander. And it always led him back to the same place.

Jules.

SCOTT CLEANED the last gun of the day while sending anxious glances through the doorway that led to the rest of the barn. He was worried that Jules would leave before he had the chance to get cleaned up. She'd been conspicuously absent from the usual staff hangouts for the past couple of days, and as soon as she disappeared after work, he wouldn't see her again until the next day.

No need to worry, though. Jules was putting away the harnesses, leaving them prepped for the next day.

A hand fell on Scott's shoulder, making him jump. "You looking forward to finally working with the guests tomorrow?"

Jimmy.

Scott turned toward his manager and forced a smile. "Sure am."

Not.

Jimmy had stressed over and over that guests overestimated their ability to do dangerous activities. They assumed that because they were on a dude ranch, repelling down the side of a barn was risk-free.

For the past two weeks, Scott had been able to go four-wheeling, shooting, hiking, fishing—every day he got to go play. Starting the next day, it would be more akin to babysitting and making sure no one died while on his watch.

Scott didn't interrupt Jimmy as he gave his best tips and tricks, even though his window was closing to be able to talk with Jules, preferably alone. He'd just managed to get on his manager's good side, though, and life had been easier since then. He'd rather not rock the boat.

By the time Jimmy had finished, Jules had disappeared. Scott didn't let his smile drop, not until after he'd thanked Jimmy for his wisdom. But when he turned, scanning the barn for any hint that Jules might still be there, disappointment settled in his gut. She'd already left.

Out of the corner of his eye, Scott swore he saw a brief flash of curly hair right outside the barn door.

Penny.

Scott thanked Jimmy again and then leaped over the desk and ran out the door. Penny and Jules were walking toward the lodge, laughing.

His steps slowed, realization settling over him.

Jules didn't need him. Not like he needed her. She was probably avoiding him because she was afraid he'd read more into the kiss than she'd intended. Scott didn't know why she'd done it in the first place, considering how often she'd made sure he knew he'd been placed in the friend zone and was staying there. But she obviously regretted the impulsive move.

Anger replaced the disappointment.

"Jules," he yelled.

Penny stopped and turned, but Jules didn't.

"You really want to have this conversation here?" Scott's voice carried further than he'd have thought possible, and it gave Jules pause.

She glanced over her shoulder. "There's nothing to say."

"I can think of a few things."

Jules looked uneasy, like she was unsure what was on his mind and wasn't thrilled at the prospect of the entire ranch hearing it. She murmured something to Penny, who then entered the lodge without her.

Jules hesitated before walking back toward Scott. They were starting to get an audience.

"I know somewhere better," he said, then nodded toward the barn. To his relief, she followed. Instead of entering the barn, however, he walked around to the side, where metal stairs wound their way up the side of the building. A platform extended from an emergency exit door on each level of the barn.

Scott walked up the stairs until he was at the highest platform. The door led to the boys' dorm. Needing a second to gather his thoughts, he sat down on one of the steps.

Jules had kept pace but chose not to sit, instead folding her arms across her chest as she walked over to a railing that wrapped around the platform. They were so high, they could see far beyond the ranch. Nothing but trees and hills and red rock for miles.

Scott had come out there each night since he'd arrived at the ranch. Armed with a headlamp, notebook, and pencil, he'd already managed to write several songs. It was amazing what some inner turmoil could do for the creative juices.

It didn't hurt that the night sky here was the most incredible thing he'd ever seen. He hadn't known that many stars existed.

Seconds ticked by, and Scott realized he had no idea what he wanted to say—or why.

Jules leaned against the railing, looking out over the mountainous desert that surrounded them. Another minute passed, and she glanced over her shoulder. "I'd really love to get a steak before the dining hall closes up—"

"Why are you mad?" Scott interrupted, finally finding his voice. "Is it because of the kiss? Or because I shot you during the paintball game?" His voice cracked on the last word. He hated that he cared so much. He wasn't used to that.

Jules slowly turned. It was another moment before she said, "The paintball game." Her words were slow, like she was having to take the time to gather them. "You said you hadn't meant to shoot me."

"Right. So the problem is..." He raised an eyebrow, urging her to finish his sentence, because if she knew it had been an accident, he was confused as to what the issue was.

"You wouldn't have if you'd known it was me."

Still not seeing the issue. "Would you rather I'd gone all Rambo on you?" he asked.

"Yes."

Scott couldn't have heard right, and he leaned forward, resting his arms on his knees. "Sorry?"

Jules released a long sigh, like she was exhausted and didn't want to be at the top of a barn having this conversation. "I already told you, I don't want you treating me like you do every other girl whose pants you're trying to get into. No meaningless compliments. No special treatment."

Annoyance bubbled up in Scott's chest. "For the record, I don't do...*that*. Is that really what you think of me?"

She paused, suddenly seeming unsure. "Your parents sent you here for a reason. And I've seen the pictures that explain why."

Scott buried his head in his hands. Yes, there were pictures. Plenty of them, thanks to the paparazzi who always seemed to catch him at his worst. Sure, Scott liked to have fun with his friends, and it usually ended with a make-out session or two, but it was just fun. Amusement. To him, kissing was no different from going to the movies. Despite how the press framed it, he didn't take it further than that.

His gaze shot up, once again angry. Scott had never met a girl who could get under his skin like this. "That makes you an expert, huh? Just like people who see the pictures of me falling in the river or belaying Penny on the rock wall will have a perfect representation of my time here at the ranch." He gave a quick shake of his head. "I'm not the guy in the pictures. And if I'm giving you special treatment, it's only because I like you. Not like the girls I meet at parties and don't ever see again. But I like, like you. And you won't let me even try."

Jules seemed to have been stunned into silence, not moving to leave but not sure what to say either. "In that paintball game, I knew that if you had shot me on purpose, I was safe," she finally said, her voice shaky. "That you weren't trying to win me over. Just seeing me as...me." Jules's hands were balled, and she shook them out, like she was forcing herself to calm down.

She sucked in a long, shuddered breath. "Guys always want the girl they can't have, and then as soon as they do, they're on to the next challenge. That's why Blair never saw me—never realized how good we'd be together. He didn't see me because the girl he wanted was the one girl he couldn't have. Not when his mother was our high school principal." She shrugged. "Joke's on me, I guess. I tried everything, including some things I'm not proud of, to make him realize what a mistake it was. It obviously didn't change a thing. Only difference is that Blair is a good guy, and he didn't leave Sandra. Because it turns out that they belong together." She gave a small, humorless laugh and then walked over and sank onto the step next to Scott.

Was that why Scott was attracted to Jules? Because she was the one girl he couldn't have? Part of him wondered, because if he was being honest, it did make her more attractive. But if she ever returned his affection, he couldn't imagine himself moving on without her. He'd be the world's biggest idiot to do something like that.

Knowing he didn't have anything to lose, Scott said, "I won't lie, you're gorgeous and your attempts to push me away only make me want to pull you closer. Can you blame me, though?" Jules's gaze snapped to him, and he continued before she could run away. One of the perks of choosing the highest platform of the barn's stairs was that it made it that much more difficult for her to leave. "But that doesn't mean that what I feel for you isn't real. You are the only reason I've been able to survive the time I have at the ranch. You and your compassion and humor and completely adorable awkwardness."

When Jules opened her mouth to protest, he held up a finger to let her know he wasn't quite done. "You worry about me giving you special treatment, but you don't need it. You can clean a gun and rappel down a mountain faster than any guy here. And even though I didn't know it was you when I shot you earlier, I can make you a promise that I'll never go easy on you. If I were to do it all over again, I would shoot you. Twice, if it meant that much to you."

Jules's expression relaxed, and she bumped him with her shoulder. "You mean that?"

Scott hesitated. He had said it, but was it something he could stick to? "When I'm with you," he said slowly, choosing his words carefully, "I can talk for hours, or sit in silence for just as long. I want to have inside jokes with you and adventures and things that no one else has but us. I'm tired of superficial. Does all of that count as special treatment?"

Silence.

And then Jules slipped her hand into his and squeezed. "I want to believe all that. I do. But whatever the truth behind those pictures in the magazines is, you can't say that you don't like having a new girl each night, people singing your praises wherever you go. And I mean that in the most literal sense."

"It was fun for the first year or so," he admitted. "But you saw what happened when I tried to do something normal. My parents wanted me to be more grounded, have a better sense of reality, but that's not what everyone else wants. They want to put me in a bubble—pretend that I don't exist in the same world they do. When those worlds collide, they don't know what to do with me. I never thought I'd feel normal again. Not until I met you."

Jules turned so she more fully faced him, her eyes searching for where the truth was hidden. "I'm sorry I've made things harder for you the past couple of days."

"It's okay," he said, his breaths now ragged. Jules was way too close, and the way her finger was sliding over his hand—it left him dizzy. Scott forced his mind to return to the conversation. "I get why you are cautious around me. Honestly, you're too good to be seen hanging out with the likes of me. I've made more bad choices than good over the past few years. Of course, you can't tell my parents that I admitted that. I'd never hear the end of it."

Jules smirked. And it was adorable. "I think I'll be the judge of that, thank you very much." The way her eyes teased him and she scooted closer—it was Scott's undoing.

He needed to take some space. Respect Jules's wishes. He'd just barely got her speaking to him again, after all.

Scott jumped up from the step, Jules's hand dropping from his. "After prepping all those harnesses, I'm sure you're starving. We better get you one of those steaks you've been wanting."

Jules studied him, her eyes reflecting surprise. "Okay."

Scott silently cursed himself. Here he'd been going on about how amazing Jules was, and she'd scooted closer in response. He was supposed to kiss her. Or at least put an arm around her. But the thought of doing that with someone he actually liked—someone who could hurt him?

He hadn't known how to handle that. Was this how everyone felt in new relationships? This uncertainty and self-doubt?

If so, he was shocked that anyone managed to get through the dating process with their sanity still intact.

Just liking a girl for two weeks, and he was barely holding his together.

12

JULIANNA

"You're doing amazing," Julianna told a young girl who couldn't be older than thirteen.

"I don't know if I can do this," the girl called down, her voice shaking. Her left hand held a rope in front of her, with her right hand pulling it behind her back, which would act as the brake when she rappelled down the side of the barn. Except she had no need for it, because there was no way she was going anywhere anytime soon.

Scott stood at the top, trying to soothe her, but it only seemed to make her more nervous.

Penny was walking past, and she threw a sympathetic glance toward the girl. "I know the feeling."

"Want to go up and talk to her? The poor girl is scared out of her mind, but she's been determined to conquer the wall for the past twenty minutes. I'm not sure Scott's the best person to help her. Pretty sure the only thing he's accomplishing is making her hands sweat more."

Penny swallowed hard. Julianna knew that the top of the barn made Penny nervous—having to climb three flights of stairs to get there—but to her credit, she gave a small nod and said, "I'll see what I can do."

She disappeared back into the barn and appeared at the top a couple of minutes later. Julianna had to bite back a smile when Penny ordered Scott to back up three steps to give them space before kneeling on the platform next to the girl. Julianna couldn't hear what was said, but whatever it was, it worked. The girl's movements were slow and halting, but ten minutes later, she'd managed to walk down the side of the rock wall.

The grin that girl wore was something Julianna would never forget. The pride that came from overcoming an obstacle lit up her eyes, and she was jumping around so much, her fist punching the air, it made it difficult for Julianna to get the harness off her.

Julianna laughed as the girl handed her the helmet. "Am I going to see you back on this thing tomorrow?"

The girl's smile dipped. "Uh..." But then it returned in full force. "Yup. Is...uh...Scott Dallenforth going to be up there again?"

"I'm not sure, but you're going to rock it either way." Julianna lowered her voice to a whisper. "Between you and me, I think you'll do even better if he's not around."

The girl scrunched her eyebrows together. "Was it that obvious that he was making me nervous?"

"He makes *everyone* nervous," Julianna said with a smile.

"Even you?"

"Even me."

"Awww, I thought we'd gotten past that stage, Jules," Scott said from just behind her, causing her to jump.

The young girl's cheeks turned a bright shade of pink, and she ran off toward a middle-aged couple who had been watching from a bench next to the barn.

"I had to say something to help that girl feel better about

things," Julianna said, turning to face Scott. Her breath caught at how close he was standing. She could see the dirt streaks from when he'd taken a group out on the four-wheelers earlier.

"Well, that's a relief," he said, pretending to wipe sweat from his forehead with the back of his hand. He grinned. "You coming camping tonight?"

Julianna cocked an eyebrow and studied Scott. This was the first she'd heard about a camping trip. And weren't they supposed to be working on the "just friends" thing? Going camping together seemed...intimate. Forget the fact that it involved sleeping in dirt and wearing enough mosquito spray that she doubted he'd want to come within six feet of her.

There were also stars and the romantic glow of a campfire. And no adult supervision.

"We have work tomorrow. Weekend isn't here for another three days," she said, her words coming out quick.

Penny walked up and must have seen the panic in Julianna's expression, because she laughed and said, "Relax. There's a bunch of people going right after dinner, and we'll be back in time for breakfast. It'll be fun."

Julianna's gaze moved from Penny to Scott, then back to Penny. "How does everyone know about this stuff except me?"

"You were out leading that hike for most of the day," Scott said. There was something about the way his eyes crinkled, and the reassuring nod, that immediately put her at ease. That made her trust him. That made her feel like she could follow him anywhere, and it would be all right.

That was a very dangerous feeling.

JULIANNA EMERGED from their apartment under the lodge, a backpack slung over one shoulder. "So, who's driving us to this thing?"

A guilty expression flashed across Penny's face, and Julianna didn't need any more info than that.

Sandra and Blair. That was who. Apparently, Sandra had bought a Suburban just before making a road trip out of coming to the ranch. It wasn't the nicest-looking thing, but it could fit eight people.

Except, Julianna didn't want to be in a Suburban with seven other people, least of all the four of them. It wasn't that they weren't nice—they were—but she'd rather they not be. Whenever Julianna was with Sandra and Blair, her breaths immediately shallowed. She hated the jealousy that still rose up, but more, she hated the guilt. They didn't know what she had done the past school year.

But she did.

And as they bounced along a dirt road toward their campsite, it gnawed at her.

"You okay?" Scott asked, placing his hand lightly on her knee. His eyebrows were knit in concern. "You look a little pale."

"Y-yeah. Just a little motion sick." Julianna was starting to feel a bit nauseous, so it wasn't a lie.

"I told you that you should have let me drive," Sandra scolded Blair through a smile. "You always take the turns too fast."

"A gentleman always drives," he said, his lips quirking up into the half-smile that Julianna had never been able to get enough of.

"And what would you know of being a gentleman?" Sandra retorted.

Okay, guess they were turning her motion sickness into a chance to flirt and exchange witty banter.

Great.

Julianna really did think she was going to puke.

"Are you sure you're okay?" Scott asked again.

Penny squeezed Julianna's arm on her other side, as if letting her know she was there for her, then folded her arms across her chest and glared toward the front row. She didn't do more, considering the three of them were squished together in the very last row of seats, but it was enough. Julianna had confided in Penny about Blair and Sandra the week before when she'd declined Sandra's invitation for a late-night swim, and just the fact that Penny was silently letting Julianna know that she had her back was enough.

The more Julianna thought about it, she didn't know why her friend had taken her side at all. It wasn't like Sandra and Blair had done anything wrong. Blair hadn't meant to break Julianna's heart, and Sandra hadn't meant to swoop in and steal something that had never belonged to Julianna in the first place.

It was Julianna who had been mean and petty.

But Penny seemed to understand everything that Julianna wasn't saying. She reached over and squeezed Julianna's arm, while Scott's gaze flicked from Julianna to Blair, then back again.

Scott leaned in close and whispered in Julianna's ear, "I told you before, I can help you get him back." His breath tickled, and Julianna had to fight back the desire it ignited in her. Good thing she had already made it clear that she was off limits. That she wasn't like all those other girls whose hearts stalled at every dimple and every stolen glance. That her heart still belonged to someone else.

"Thank you." She gave him a sad smile. "But there's nothing to fight for. He doesn't see me. Not really. Not like I see him. Saw him. Used to—kinda still do." She released a sigh. "I don't even know anymore."

"And you think he does? High school boys don't have a clue." Scott said it as if he were on a loftier plane than boys like Blair—like he hadn't just graduated high school himself.

It was adorable.

"Got that right," Penny said with a satisfied nod, and she and Scott fist-bumped.

"He doesn't know what he wants," Scott said, his tone firm.

Julianna would have given anything to hear those words just a few months earlier.

Now?

They made her sick to her stomach.

"Please don't say that," she said, her voice so soft, she didn't know if he'd heard her.

"Why not?"

It was a simple question, but Julianna knew it was going to have a complicated answer—one that she was still trying to figure out. And thank goodness she wasn't going to have to come up with one that made sense, because the Suburban abruptly stopped, throwing them all forward. Blair backed up a couple of feet, then turned off on an even narrower dirt road. Up ahead, several other cars were parked next to a clearing.

"Safe and sound. Just like I told you," Blair said, throwing Sandra a grin. She rolled her eyes but was laughing at the same time.

"Barely." Sandra jumped from the Suburban and opened the sliding side door. "Ride's over, folks. Once you get out, turn to your left if you managed to make it through relatively unscathed. To your right are some bushes if Blair's driving left you a little worse for wear."

"No one's going to puke," Blair said, jumping from the driver's seat.

"Actually..." His best friend, Cameron, then slid out of the side of the vehicle and stumbled to the designated puking bush.

Sandra shot Blair an I-told-you-so look.

Blair raised a shoulder and grinned. "He's always had a sensitive stomach."

"Which only seems to be sensitive around you," Cameron called before returning to his bush.

Julianna slid out of the Suburban after Amanda and grabbed her stuff from the back. "I didn't bring much. Just a sleeping bag, a pillow, and a toothbrush. Think I should have brought more?"

Penny grabbed her sleeping bag, tucked a pillow under one arm, and followed Julianna. "That's all I brought. Figured we'd get back in time to clean up and grab breakfast." She held up her tooth-brush. "This is just in case...you know..." Pink crept up her cheeks. "Well, it was Andy that invited me. Or at least, he's the one who told me about it. Which is kind of the same thing as an invitation—"

"Who's Andy?" Julianna interrupted. Penny was the closest thing Julianna had to a best friend, and she didn't even know that Penny had a crush? What kind of friend did that make Julianna?

Penny's blush deepened. "He's on maintenance duty, so kind of keeps to himself." She pointed to a tall redhead that Julianna had seen in passing. He was setting up some logs for a fire, while everyone else watched. "He's a good guy. Funny too, once you get to know him."

"It looks like he could use some help with the fire," Scott said.

Julianna started, not realizing he'd been standing just behind her. He gave Penny a pointed look.

"Oh, I-I don't know anything about campfires." Julianna didn't often see Penny at a loss of words, but she was sure strug-gling to come up with an excuse right now.

Scott laughed. "Neither does he, by the looks of it. But he's trying when no one else is, which says something about the guy."

Penny nodded slowly. "Okay. Yeah. And it's not like I don't

know the guy. I talk to him every time he comes through the barn to fix a lightbulb. It won't be weird. Not at all." And she was back to rambling.

"Just go," Julianna said with a laugh, and she gave her friend a little nudge.

After another minute of hesitation, and then slowly leaning her sleeping bag against a tree and balancing her pillow on top, Penny glanced at Andy. If she had been hoping that he'd have the fire going by the time she'd painstakingly set her belongings down, she'd have been disappointed, because Andy was nowhere closer to having that fire lit.

"Going to help with the campfire now," she muttered, as if giving herself a pep talk. "I shouldn't be nervous. It's not like I'm asking him to make out with me. But maybe I should brush my teeth first, just in case."

And she continued to talk to herself like that all the way over to the campfire.

"Glad it's not just us guys that feel like we're constantly tripping over our own feet," Scott said with a smile. "It usually feels like you girls have it all figured out and you've somehow managed to become the puppet master, holding the strings. Like you know if you give a smile in a certain way, it will make me scoot closer. Or if you rub your arms on a cold night, I'll offer my jacket."

The way Scott was looking at her—his gaze piercing—left Julianna wondering if he was talking generically, or when he said "you" he really was talking about her.

His eyes in that moment—they were honest. Searching. Vulnerable. And she felt her resolve crumbling. Not completely, just enough to scare her.

"Well, I guess I should find me a good sleeping spot," Julianna said, readjusting her grip on her sleeping bag and pillow and surveying the clearing. "Do you think anyone happened to think of a tarp?"

Scott seemed startled by the abrupt shift of mood, and disappointed. "Um...maybe. I don't know. All I brought was a sleeping bag. Forgot to even grab a pillow." He busied himself looking at the ground. "Maybe if I can just find a soft enough rock..."

Julianna knew what she should do, but she hesitated. She'd known Scott was different than she'd expected since the hike they'd taken on their third day at the ranch. But she kept treating him as if he were exactly what he presented himself to be—a shallow rock star. A player. Someone to be careful around.

"You can share mine," she said, her words escaping too quickly. Otherwise, they may have never escaped at all.

Scott's gaze snapped up, and he raised an eyebrow, like he didn't think he'd heard right.

"Your...."

Ugh. He was going to make her say it. Fine.

"My pillow. We can share. What kind of friend would I be if I let you sleep with your face in the dirt?"

"That's nice of you. Thanks. You're a great...friend."

The way he said it, it seemed like Scott didn't like the word "friend" much. And truth be told, seeing Penny and Andy sharing shy smiles as they worked together to get the fire going, neither did she.

13

SCOTT

So. It was official. Scott had been friend-zoned. He'd known but hadn't been ready to give up hope. He hadn't exactly been helping his case when he offered to help Julianna get Blair back. He'd wanted to see her reaction, though—gauge her response so he would know if she was really that hung up on the guy.

Sure, the guy was buff, and girls probably thought he was good-looking. But what did that guy have that Scott didn't?

A normal high school experience, that was what. From what Jules had told Scott, Blair had been on the swim team. They had worked on a school project together. She'd nearly asked him to one of the school dances but had chickened out at the last moment.

Blair was relatable.

Scott was the guy that was so out of touch with reality that girls could imagine flings with him, but not more. How could they when he himself lost track of what state he was in, and where he'd be a week later? He'd been fine with that kind of life, to be honest. All the benefits without the consequences.

But now?

He was starting to care. He was starting to want to have something beyond one night.

The problem was that Scott was beginning to have different expectations of himself—of relationships—but no one else was. They still thought of him as the player.

He knew it had been desperate, purposely leaving his pillow back at the ranch, and then hoping it wouldn't backfire.

But if he could get Jules in a situation where she couldn't run away like she always did, maybe he could get her to see that side of him.

The real side.

The side that hadn't come out since he and his friends had been discovered playing rock music in his garage.

But he couldn't do that when he was sitting sadly next to a campfire that he hadn't even realized existed until that moment. Andy and Penny had finally got it going after trying for the better part of an hour—thanks to someone remembering they had some lighter fuel in the back of their car. Guess the guy really hadn't known how to start a fire.

Everyone surrounding Scott was laughing and talking, goofing off, but he just stared into the flames. He wiped his palms on the sides of his pants. Could they hear the thumping of his heart against his ribcage?

He could.

His gaze found Jules, sitting on the opposite side of the fire. She wasn't goofing off with everyone else. Like him, she sat alone. Quiet. And her gaze was on him.

Maybe people back home were right. He'd changed. And not for the better. His friends too. He wondered if it was too late to go back to who he had been—what he had been.

Scott knew what he needed.

Music.

It was the one thing that helped him anymore.

He'd spotted a guitar lying on a tree stump, and he asked if anyone minded if he borrowed it for a bit. No one answered, so Scott took the guitar back to where he'd already laid out his sleeping bag. He sat down and leaned against a fallen tree, plucking at a few strings and playing a couple of chords to see if it was in tune.

And then he sang.

It wasn't a song that he'd recorded, or one that he'd slaved over for days and weeks, trying to find something he thought the recording studio would approve of.

It was impromptu, and it held all the grief and longing and love that had been dormant for so long, he'd forgotten they existed.

When he finished, silence sat heavy among the trees. Scott realized that everyone had stopped talking—that they were all listening. And he hadn't noticed that sometime while he had been singing, Jules had come over and sat on the sleeping bag next to him. Her eyes were moist.

No one said anything. Like they didn't dare to. There were no phones out this time—no cameras. Like they had all forgotten about them.

This would be the first time Scott could be accused of breaking up a party, and he realized how dumb it had been to pull out the guitar and sing, as if he were alone. Just because he needed some music therapy didn't mean that everyone else wanted to be a part of it.

"That was incredible," Jules said, breaking the silence. As if that were a cue, everyone slowly turned away and went back to what they were doing. The chatter rose to its original volume, though not without several backward glances.

Scott gave Jules an embarrassed smile and set the guitar back down where he'd found it. He pulled out a twenty and stuck it in between the strings as a rental fee and a thank you.

"I don't get to play for me very often," he said, returning to the sleeping bag. "Always what other people want me to play. Whatever is going to make money."

"Why can't you have both?"

He sighed. "According to the record label, it has something to do with market trends. Which I don't fall into."

Jules stared. "Are you kidding me? You just captivated an entire campsite. How can that not be in line with whatever these 'market trends' are?" She did air quotes around the last part.

Scott laughed and scooted so his and Jules's sides were touching. He hesitated, then took her hand in his. "There's something about the ambience of a campfire that lends emotion to music. But imagine hearing that over the radio while driving to school with your friends, or at a party. No one wants this kind of stuff."

Jules intertwined her fingers with his and squeezed. "That's the problem. People are afraid of feeling—of showing emotion. But you could help do something about that." She tilted her face toward the sky and shouted, "Free us from our emotional constipation, Scott Dallenforth." She paused, then burst out laughing. "Can you pretend I didn't just do that?" She made a sound he thought was supposed to indicate they were rewinding time, but it sounded more like a broken robot. "Free us, Scott Dallenforth. You're our only hope."

Scott laughed as Jules frowned.

"You're right. Too cliché." She heaved a dramatic sigh. "The point is, that was one of the most beautiful things I've ever heard. Most real, too. And music like that shouldn't be hidden just because a fat guy in a suit says it doesn't meet market trends. The guy must be emotionally dead to not be moved by that song."

It was cute the way she was getting all riled up, ready to take on his recording studio. Maybe he should hire *her* to be his manager. "My contact at the studio is actually a woman, and she hasn't heard that song. No one has. I made it up on the spot. Don't know if I could even play it again."

Jules yelped. "Are you serious?" She jumped up from the sleeping bag, causing a few heads to turn, then grabbed a backpack from behind the log.

"Coming to the rescue with your toothbrush?" Scott teased.

"Not yet. My phone to record you. Though with us sharing a pillow tonight, I may need to sacrifice my toothbrush for the greater good, considering you didn't bother bringing your own."

"I have naturally minty breath," Scott said, attempting to sound offended. It had exactly the effect he'd hoped for.

Jules smiled and sat back down next to him. "I'll be the judge of that."

"And how do you plan on doing that? I have a thing where I don't like people smelling my breath. Makes me feel weird." He cocked an eyebrow and gave her a crooked grin, knowing he was going into dangerous territory. Not only was he flirting, which was a sure way to scare her away, but he had subconsciously moved toward her and grabbed her hand again while doing it.

Her smile flickered. Her gaze searching.

Oh, crap.

Why couldn't he just not flirt with a pretty girl? Why did he always jump to this stage of things, even when he knew he shouldn't?

Scott could give a crap explanation about biology, but he knew it had nothing to do with that. At least, not in this case.

It was because Jules wasn't just any pretty girl.

She was the only one who left him tongue-tied, searching for words. The only one who kept him up at night, his thoughts unable to settle on anything, or anyone, else. The only one who made him second-guess himself.

"You're the only one who sees me," Scott murmured.

He froze. He hadn't meant to say that part out loud. Two vulnerable moments in the past ten minutes—he didn't like this feeling. Like he was losing control.

But then Jules did something unexpected.

She smiled. It was soft, like she understood what he was trying to say—or not trying to say.

"Maybe that's because I'm the only one you've allowed to see you."

And then she kissed him. But it wasn't like at the paintball field—impulsive.

This time, Jules took her time, placing a hand behind his neck. She pulled him in closer, and he readjusted his position so he leaned against the fallen tree.

When their lips met, there weren't fireworks. There was an orchestra. Every movement deliberate, and beautiful. Their lips waltzed together as her hand combed through his hair. His breath hitched. Scott had never had a kiss like this before—one that mirrored the emotions he'd expressed in his song minutes before.

A kiss that meant so much that the only way to express it was through music, because words would never be enough.

Scott didn't know how long they sat pressed up against that tree, but when they finally pulled away, nothing in the world mattered. There was only Jules. And him. And the music they'd created together.

His breaths came ragged, and Jules seemed similarly short of breath.

"That was…" She didn't finish, so Scott finished for her.

"Yeah."

And then they both laughed.

"Guess sharing a pillow tonight just got a lot more awkward," Scott said, rubbing the back of his neck.

Jules snuggled in close and leaned a head on his shoulder. "Nah. You were right about having naturally minty breath."

He smiled and rested his head on top of hers.

Whatever was happening here—he didn't know if it could last. But right then, he didn't care.

Because finally, for the first time in a long time, he understood happiness.

14

JULIANNA

Julianna woke early, the sun just starting to appear from behind the trees. Scott still slept next to her, his lips slightly parted and drool resting on his chin.

She wanted to capture that moment, afraid she'd never see it again. Or experience a kiss like the evening before.

It hadn't been her first kiss. There had been one other in tenth grade. But it had been a dare. One that the boy's friends had given him.

He'd won ten bucks off that kiss.

This one, though...holy camoly.

If anyone ever asked about her first kiss, she was going to tell them about this one. Because it was the first one that meant anything. And everything. And stole her breath.

Even though it had been she who had crazily made the first move, Julianna no longer doubted Scott or his intentions. That had not been the kiss of someone who was playing her. It was the kiss of someone who was playing for keeps.

She didn't know how long that would be—she was a realist, after all. Julianna still needed to figure out what she was doing with her life, and Scott had a world tour to go on that fall. She may have been on his website more than a few times since he'd arrived at the ranch. And a hundred times before that.

But his band's website was all show—all glam. It focused on how unbelievably attractive he and his bandmates were. But it could never capture the true essence of who Scott Dallenforth was.

The funny, compassionate, sensitive musician she was lucky enough to be able to spend the rest of the summer with.

"You're awake early." Scott had woken and was watching her, his lips twisted up into a half-smile.

"Sorry, I wasn't staring," Julianna said quickly, though realizing she'd been doing exactly that. Staring off into space, not completely aware of what she was looking at, her thoughts taking her places she'd never thought she'd go. "Not on purpose, anyway."

He pushed himself up and propped his head up on one hand. "I don't mind you staring, as long as I'm offered the same courtesy."

Julianna's cheeks warmed and she glanced down, tucking a lock of hair behind her ear. "I have bedhead, and I'm sure my mascara is running and—"

Scott interrupted her by leaning forward and placing his lips on hers. "You're beautiful," he whispered against her lips. "So stop making excuses for yourself. It's not your fault if all the other girls wish they could be you."

"They do not." She gave Scott a playful nudge.

"Awww...you two are so cute," Penny said, flopping over in her sleeping bag on Julianna's other side. Her curly hair was usually a bit of a mess, but this morning had taken things to a new level. Julianna wouldn't have been surprised to find at least three squirrels nestled up inside. "Do you mind being cute quietly, though? Some of us didn't get to sleep as early as you."

Julianna wouldn't have considered her and Scott's night

early, considering they had been talking until three in the morning. But to Penny's credit, she'd had yet to come to bed before they had drifted off.

"Wish we could," Scott said while glancing at his phone. "But breakfast at the lodge starts in twenty minutes. So much for showering before work this morning."

Julianna groaned. "Good thing we work at a ranch where some level of filthiness is expected." Scott sat up, and she saw he had a long patch of dirt that spread from his neck up through his hair on one side. She snorted. "Of course, I think they have standards that might not be met today."

He raised an eyebrow and then craned his neck as he searched himself, trying to see what Julianna saw. "What?"

"Nothing."

Penny sat up and stretched. "I bet I could plant a garden in that 'nothing' up the side of your head."

"It would go well with the petting zoo you got going in your hair," he retorted as he resumed his search for what he was obviously missing. Penny just laughed.

It took the better part of those twenty minutes to wake everyone up and get Blair walking in a straight enough line that he felt he was awake enough to drive.

"Maybe I should drive," Scott suggested.

Sandra seemed okay with that idea, her eyes lighting up, but Blair bristled and stuck out his chest, suddenly seeming much more awake. "I got it, but thanks anyway."

Scott raised a shoulder, like he didn't care either way, and jumped into the back seat of the Suburban.

Blair seemed to care more about the interaction than Scott had and took the dirt road back to the ranch faster than he had on his way to the campground.

"Want to try slowing down?" Amanda asked, her voice shaky.

Julianna noticed that everyone in the vehicle was holding on to something.

"Got to get back in time for work," Blair said with a grunt. "Hopefully the dining hall will still be open and we can at least grab an apple or something."

Sandra laid a hand on his arm. "But it's not worth—"

Her words cut off when the back of the Suburban fishtailed as they rounded a bend. Blair tried to regain control but overcorrected and sent them up a bank, where the front wheels hit a tree. Better that than the drop-off on the opposite side of the road.

Unfortunately, the tree acted like a lever, making the vehicle tilt up and backwards. Julianna grabbed the seat in front of her and glanced at Scott and Penny, their wide eyes matching hers.

Julianna didn't remember much after that. Not until she was hanging upside down by her seatbelt.

"Everyone okay?" Blair called.

They all seemed to be, though Julianna felt lightheaded, and she could hear that someone was still pressing down on the accelerator, the rev of the engine making her anxious. "Blair, you gotta turn it off."

"Right." He turned the key, and silence settled over them. It was worse than the noise from the engine.

"I need to get out of here," Julianna mumbled.

As she moved to unbuckle her seatbelt, Scott said, "Wait."

It was too late, though, and when she pressed the button to unbuckle the belt, she fell to the roof of the vehicle.

Oh, right. Gravity.

In her panic, Julianna had forgotten she was hanging upside down.

It took some scrambling and a bruised knee, but she got the side door open and stumbled out into the sunshine.

Sandra appeared through the passenger door a moment

later. "Are you okay?" she asked. "I could have opened that for you from the outside." She was looking at Julianna so kindly that Julianna felt guilty about the things she'd said about Sandra. She'd always known that underneath all the skulls and spiked bracelets was someone Julianna might have been friends with if they hadn't fallen for the same guy.

Except, Sandra was better. And Blair had been right about choosing her.

Maybe it was the fact that Julianna was still struggling to stand and that Sandra was helping her walk over to a large rock at the edge of the road. Or maybe it was because they'd just had a near-death experience. But before Julianna thought better of it, she blurted out, "It was me."

Sandra raised an eyebrow and adjusted her spiked bracelets that kept slipping. "No, that was all Blair. I think he was jealous of your new boyfriend and had something to prove. Boys can be so dumb sometimes." She laughed, and it only made Julianna feel worse.

Julianna sucked in a deep breath as she sank onto the rock. "No, I mean, it was me who spread those pictures last year. Of you and Blair. It's because of me that Principal Howell found out about you two. I mean, how his mom found out."

"Oh." Sandra's eyebrows shot up, and Julianna braced herself for Sandra's anger. Except it never came. Instead, her lips quirked up at the edges, and she sat on the rock next to Julianna. "You're the last person I would have ever suspected."

"That's because you didn't know I existed." Julianna shouldn't have said that part. High school was over. A post-school pity party wasn't what anyone needed. She watched as the rest of their group made their way out of the Suburban. A car lumbered up—more kids from the ranch, and they were talking to Blair. One was pulling out a phone.

"You're not wrong," Sandra said. "I had my little group of friends and didn't really know anyone outside of it. The only reason I met Blair was because he was best friends with Amanda's boyfriend. Never stopped to think what it was like for someone who didn't already have their own group. Not unless they were literally thrown into my path." She paused. "I hate to ask, but why did you do it?"

Julianna gave a humorless laugh. "Why does a high school girl do anything? To try to get the boy she likes to notice her."

At least, that had been the way it was for Julianna. Maybe others weren't quite so desperate.

Sandra turned her gaze to her spiked bracelets. "I get that. And I'm sorry."

"Hey, I'm the one apologizing here," Julianna said, sitting up straight. "I was selfish, and I never got to know you beyond the spikes."

"Join the club," Sandra muttered. "Not many people do."

Julianna gave a quick shake of her head. "The point is that he totally made the right choice. Not that there was a choice, but if there had been, you're it. You're the one for him. And it took us coming here for me to realize it."

Sandra shot Julianna a side smile. "No hard feelings. Seriously. It was better that his mom knew. Who knows, if she hadn't found out, maybe we wouldn't have had a happy ending." She glanced toward the upside-down Suburban and groaned. "I better get over there. I can read Blair's moods, and right now he's beating himself up about this."

It wasn't another minute after Sandra left that Scott joined Julianna on the rock. "You okay?"

The fact that people kept asking probably meant that she wasn't. Her gaze dropped. "Sorry, I kind of panicked there. I took off and didn't even check on you and Penny."

Scott placed a finger under her chin and lifted it so their

gazes met. "Don't worry about us. It's you that we're concerned about."

Moisture pricked at her eyes. "I've never been in a car accident before."

"Me neither."

Then he wrapped his arm around her shoulders, and they sat in silence. She didn't need him to say anything—his presence was enough.

15

SCOTT

Scott pestered Jules all day, asking if she was okay. It got to the point that she got mad at him for asking. It was like she wanted to pretend nothing had happened—like it was just a normal day on the ranch.

Once they'd gotten rides back and given statements to Jimmy and Kat, Jules had insisted she could still do her job. So even though Blair, Sandra, Amanda, and Cameron had claimed they needed the day off (and yet somehow had been well enough to drive down to Lake Powell), Scott had said he was fine too. Anything if it meant being able to spend more time with Jules.

It turned out, however, that not many guests were interested in the activities he had been assigned to for the day. This meant a lot of downtime and mundane tasks. And a lot of time to think.

He'd tried to keep his focus on the world tour he'd be leaving for at the end of the summer, and how he was already a third done with his time at the ranch. Another month and a half and he'd be a free man.

Which made him think about how he only had another six weeks with Jules. Had she been thinking of their kiss from the previous evening as much as he had? They hadn't spoken about it since. Did she regret it? That led him to wonder if she'd be interested in doing some traveling with him. Then realize he had no idea if that was something she'd enjoy doing. Scott really didn't know her at all. And vice versa. He was pretty sure she still saw him as the rock star who had been forced into a cowboy hat and a plaid shirt—someone she couldn't take seriously.

Which led him to a plan for how he was going to prove her wrong.

———

AN ABANDONED BARN SAT at the edge of the ranch. Scott had discovered it when one of his guests had gone wandering off by the stables after getting bored with the archery range. And in that two-story barn were a stage and an outdated dance floor that had been used at some point in the distant past. It sat on the second level, sound speakers long forgotten, tables and chairs covered in dust.

And this was where Scott was going to prove that he was the man for Jules, whether she liked to admit it or not.

It didn't take much to get Penny and Andy on board, and between the three of them, the stage was set. Figuratively, and literally.

It was five o'clock when Scott strolled down the stairs of the activity barn after having just sent a family down the zipline. His pulse was too quick, his hands too moist. He'd never been this nervous to talk to a girl before. Would she like the surprise?

Penny leaned against the rec desk. Her gaze flitted to him, then back to Jules, who was putting away some gear in the back room. This was the part where Penny was supposed to ask Jules if she'd like to go on a tractor ride. She had connections now that she was dating Andy, who worked with the big machinery as part of his job.

Scott had been worried that Jules would think the idea was lame, but even from across the barn, where he had paused on the steps, he could see her eyes light up. And then she went into turbo mode, like she wanted to get done as quickly as possible.

Shoot. He hoped that Andy and Penny could slow her down, because he needed to get out to the abandoned barn before they did. He'd been hoping to change his clothes first, but now he didn't think he had time. Not when he needed to grab the food that should be waiting for him in the kitchen, hopefully without raising too many eyebrows. Another one of Andy's connections.

Scott, however, did nothing but raise eyebrows, and when he started taking the food that had been left for him in an old-fashioned picnic basket, the kitchen staff pestered him with questions, as if he were trying to use his celebrity status to get extra privileges.

Thankfully, Andy came to his rescue before rushing out to prep the tractor for the scenic tour he was planning on taking Penny and Jules on.

Scott didn't know why the guy was helping him, but he had a strong feeling that it had to do with Penny. And Scott was totally okay with using it to his advantage. He had his own girl to win over, after all.

THE RUMBLE of the tractor grew closer, and Scott straightened the already straight napkins. He had thought about candles, but instead went with the Christmas lights that still decorated the walls around the dance floor. Sure, it was midsummer, but they offered a romantic feeling to the room. And he could use all the help he could get.

When he heard the tractor stop, Scott grabbed the bandana

he'd stuffed in his back pocket and took the steps two at a time. One step shifted under his foot and sent him stumbling. Luckily he'd taken a few parkour classes and was able to do a roll that ended with him back on his feet.

"This place is kinda creepy," he heard Jules say. Yikes. Hopefully she wouldn't think so by the time the evening ended. He appeared in the doorway of the barn just as Penny and Andy were leaping back into the tractor and Jules was looking around, bewildered, saying, "You're just going to leave me here?"

"Don't worry, I can give you a ride back," Scott said.

Jules spun and faced him, her lips parted in surprise. "The tractor ride was just so they could get me out here." She said it matter-of-factly, no question. Scott had used her friends to trick her into meeting him. Hopefully this didn't turn out to be a big mistake.

"Thought you'd like a tour of the place." Scott lifted the bandana. "Of course, I will need to blindfold you before going in."

Jules blinked. And then blinked again. "You want to give me a tour...blindfolded. Of a haunted barn."

"It will be worth it. Trust me."

And then Scott worried that she didn't trust him, and that that was the problem. It was the reason he'd felt compelled to trick her into meeting him for a romantic evening—so he could show her the real him. Not the one she thought she knew. He was the guitar-strumming guy from the night before, not the rock star everyone saw him as, and he was here to prove it.

And then Jules smiled. It was the type of smile that said she did trust him. And that she wanted to be there with him, haunted barn or not. She closed her eyes. "Just to let you know, If I hear anything creepy or feel something run past my leg, I am so out of here."

"And I'll be right behind you."

The edges of Jules's lips twitched up, and she squeezed her eyes even tighter, which only made Scott like her more, and made him more nervous. He fumbled with the bandana as he attempted to tie it around the back of Jules's head, but he managed to finally get it, and only pulled out three hairs in the process.

"Watch your step," he said as he led her into the barn and to the stairs that would take them to the second floor. Halfway up, when Jules had tripped on a wobbly step and then hit her shin on the one above it, Scott thought that maybe he should have thought this through.

But when she got to the top and he took the bandana off, seeing her expression—it was all worth it. At least for him. She might not agree, depending on how big a bruise she ended up with the next day.

Jules didn't say anything at first but simply took it all in. The white Christmas lights that adorned the rustic beams (because saying old, rotting wood didn't sound quite as romantic), the plaid tablecloth that he'd laid on the floor to act as a picnic blanket, and the basket that sat in the middle of it.

"When did you have time to do all this?" she asked, turning to him.

Scott grinned. "I had some help." He then took Jules by the hand and led her to the blanket. His guitar sat to the side of it, resting in its stand. "Would you like some music to accompany your meal?"

Jules sat on the blanket, her legs to the side and her hands resting on top—all proper-like. She tilted her head to the side and said sheepishly, "Do you mind if we eat first? Andy took us all over the ranch in that tractor, to places I didn't even know existed, and I'm starving."

Thank goodness. He was all for romance, but his own stomach was protesting their delayed dinner. "Absolutely." He reached into the basket and pulled out chicken salad sand-wiches, grapes, and mini tarts for dessert. Scott had thought there'd be more, but he supposed he should be grateful that Andy had been able to grab what he had.

If Jules was bothered by the lack of choices, she didn't show it. Instead, she ate three sandwiches, half the grapes, and four tarts.

Scott had never been out with a girl who felt comfortable enough to eat in front of him. Usually they ordered an expensive salad, then poked at it for the entire night, either because they were too nervous to eat in front of him or they were afraid they'd end up with leaves stuck between their teeth.

Not Jules, though. She seemed to forget he was even there until she was licking lemon custard off her fingers. When she realized he'd only made it through half as much as she had and was watching her with an amused smile, pink tinged her cheeks.

"Um... I..." She raised a shoulder. "I guess I was even hungrier than I realized."

"Making sure guests don't shoot themselves while at the gun range can do that to a person."

Jules placed a hand on his arm and smiled, and Scott couldn't help but mirror it. "What you've done here is amazing."

"I wanted you to see me outside work. Wanted to give you the chance to ask me anything—get to know the real me."

Jules leaned back on her arms and studied him for a moment. "Why?"

"Because you don't trust me. You think your future lies with someone like Blair—someone who isn't good enough for you."

"And you are?" She sat up, her gaze curious.

Scott hesitated. That was a good question. Was he good enough for Jules? Before arriving at the ranch, he wouldn't have given her a second glance. It didn't matter who you were, just to be able to spend a few hours in his company was an honor. But being forced to be out there at the ranch for the past few weeks? It had changed things.

He now realized he'd been wrong.

And if someone like Jules even gave him a chance, he'd be lucky.

"I'd like to try—if you'll let me."

Jules seemed confused by the request. "I thought last night was a one-time thing—your reputation precedes you, and I knew not to expect more." Her eyebrows furrowed in the center. "Are you messing with me? Because if you are—"

"I'm not," Scott interrupted. "I would never do that." Even as he said it, he knew she had every reason to be suspicious. He'd certainly made a point of posting pictures of a different girl in his arms every night on his social media. Funnily enough, he'd actually had a couple of long-term girlfriends over the past few years, but when he posted pictures of dozens of girls, the paparazzi could never figure out which one it was. They didn't even suspect he could be capable of having a long-term relationship. Of course, he had been dating both of the long-term girlfriends at the same time, so maybe he wasn't.

That didn't alleviate his desire to try. He no longer wanted to date just anyone.

Scott wanted to date Jules. And only her.

16

JULIANNA

Julianna didn't know what to make of Scott. The night before, he'd been so real—so raw. That could be the only explanation for why they had kissed the way they had, and how he'd sung as if nothing else mattered.

And then he'd had her friends practically kidnap her—okay, she had gone willingly, but now she couldn't think of a plausible explanation for why she had agreed to a ride on a tractor without even questioning it. Because, seriously, if she'd thought about it for longer than a second, she would have realized that she was going as a third wheel. And no one wants that.

But now, with the lights and the food and the blanket—he was trying. And it seemed to be the real him, not the Scott Dallenforth that everyone else seemed to think they knew. Because that guy would have been dressed up in some ridiculous outfit, throwing money on a butler and a pristine location and caviar or something.

Not in his dirty work clothes, eating chicken salad sandwiches in a rundown barn.

And she couldn't think of anything she'd have liked better.

"What is your favorite color?" Scott asked her as he stood

and stretched out his legs. He then held out a hand to Julianna to help her stand. She hadn't realized how cramped her legs were until she tried using them and they immediately buckled. Scott tightened an arm around her waist and held her until she could find her feet again.

"Um...blue. No, pink. Pink and blue. But not combined. Though, maybe in a design, with a little white splashed in there."

Really? She couldn't answer a question as simple as what her favorite color was? She was hopeless.

"What about you?" she asked, not sure how their conversation had regressed to the point of asking about each other's favorite colors.

"Orange."

"Only orange? No accent colors?"

Scott walked over to a stage that lined one side of the room and hopped onto it so that he sat on the edge. "Isn't one enough?"

"For some people." Julianna walked over and hopped up next to him.

"Fine. Orange and lime green."

Julianna wrinkled her nose, then laughed. "That's quite the combination."

"Favorite movie?"

She didn't answer right away, instead focused on the movement of their feet, which had since synchronized. It wasn't that she didn't know what her favorite movie was, but she didn't understand why Scott was asking. "Why all the questions?"

Scott's movements slowed, and he looked at her, uncertainty etched in his expression. "Because I've never known any of this stuff with girls I've dated. I've never known the little things— what their favorite color was, if they preferred the ocean or the desert, or even if they had brothers or sisters. They've always just been a distraction—a ticket to a good time." He paused, then jumped from the stage. "Man, I really sound like the world's biggest jerk, don't I? I told you you're too good for me." He moved toward the picnic blanket he'd laid out. He started collecting the trash and shoving it back into the picnic basket.

This was definitely the guy from the night before, and the guy from the hiking trip through the Narrows. The guy she was falling for. The guy who wasn't the biggest jerk in the world, but the one she couldn't stop thinking about. The one she didn't want to be without.

"The ocean," she called after him. He paused. "And I'm an only child. No siblings." Scott turned toward her, and she jumped from the stage. "My favorite movie is *Rocketman*—not the one about Elton John. An old nineties slapstick comedy that I watch anytime I need a reason to smile."

She moved toward Scott, who was watching her with a look of incredulous wonder. "I can't open biscuit cans—you know, the pressurized kind you have to unwrap and press with a spoon. I never know when the stupid thing is going to pop, and I have to have someone else do it. Can't even be in the same room when they pop it open."

Julianna now stood directly in front of him. She took both his hands in hers. "And my two favorite things about being at the ranch are being able to shoot things, and spending time with you."

Scott's lips twitched up into a half-smile. "What do you say we get out of here? I have something I want to show you."

17

JULIANNA

Julianna stared at the bottom of Penny's bunk, her arms behind her head. It was late. She glanced at her phone. 2:00 a.m.

She knew she had to work in the morning. Her mind didn't care, though. It raced, going over every moment of the evening. Every movement.

After they'd left the barn, Scott had told her to change into her swimsuit and meet him at the pool. She hadn't questioned him, because if she got to see him wet, and without a shirt, she was all for it.

By the time she'd arrived, he'd been there, shirt still on, unfortunately, setting up the movie projector they'd used for pool parties.

No one else had been around, and Scott had invited her to join him in the hot tub. That was when the shirt had come off. The wait had totally been worth it.

And on the white screen Scott had set up had appeared the opening scene from *Rocketman*.

When she'd turned to him in disbelief, he'd said it was also his favorite movie and he'd brought it with him, just in case.

Because, like her, it made him happy. Helped him laugh when nothing else worked. And then they'd cuddled for the next couple of hours, laughing hysterically, enjoying each other's company.

There had been no kissing—no repeats of the previous night.

It had been better.

JULIANNA SHOULD HAVE BEEN SCARED. She didn't want to fall for someone who would never care for her in the same way she cared for him. She didn't want a repeat of Blair. Having to see him and Sandra together every day—it was killing her. Or at least it had been. Until she'd realized that Sandra wasn't the villain that Julianna had made her out to be.

And until she'd started falling for Scott Dallenforth.

There. She'd admitted it. Despite her best efforts, Julianna was falling for the rock star.

But that was the problem. It was happening all over again. That thing Julianna had said about falling for the one person you can't have? She wasn't immune. First it had been Blair, and now it was Scott.

Which was why she needed to keep her distance.

This was supposed to be a summer of self-discovery, of getting away from all the drama back home and discovering who she was without all that.

And yet, she couldn't stop thinking of Scott and how he had looked at her that evening. How he had told her things no one else ever had. And she wanted to believe all of it. Julianna desperately wanted it to all be true.

But she was afraid to hope. Afraid of what it would mean if someone like Scott truly cared for someone like her.

Julianna sat up quickly, her head brushing the wood slat

above her. Whew, that had been close. She'd already hit her head on it twice, and she didn't want to make it three.

She slipped on a pair of sandals that sat next to the bed and grabbed a light sweater, just in case.

When she stepped outside, it turned out that she didn't need it. It was the perfect summer evening, and the stars had really outdone themselves.

Julianna didn't know where she was going, only that she'd needed to get out of that stuffy apartment. She was glad she had. It was amazing out there. Nights like this—it was exactly the reason she had left home. It wasn't that they didn't have stars or beautiful things back home. But it wasn't so peaceful. Like the whole world was holding its breath, wondering what was going to happen next.

Julianna didn't realize where her feet were taking her until she was already halfway across the field.

The paintball shed was barely visible, the crescent moon giving very little light. Somehow she could feel its location, and her instinct took her straight to it. It was when she was only a couple of feet away that someone spoke.

"You couldn't sleep either, huh?"

Julianna jumped, her heart beating so fast, it felt like it would explode out of her chest. It was another moment before she managed, "Hi, Scott."

"What brings you out here so late?"

She couldn't see Scott well, but a dark outline stood out against the rest of the shed. She stepped forward, her hands out. When she made contact with the rough wood, she turned and pushed herself up onto the ledge that protruded over the dirt.

"I know I should be sleeping, but the rest of me hasn't been cooperating. Figured a little walk might help."

That's right, evade the real question of what had been keeping her up. Because there was no way she could tell Scott it was him that had been on her mind. That would only compli-cate an already complicated friendship. It was still a friendship, right? Not to mention make her sound like all the other starstruck crazies at the ranch.

"What's on your mind?" he asked.

"You."

That one word shot out before Julianna could stop it. She'd had only one thing to keep to herself, and her poor impulse control had let her down, once again. The same lack of impulse control that had made her kiss Scott. Twice.

Was she always this bad, or only around a hot rock star, who also happened to have a sensitive side and turned out was a really good friend?

Friend.

If she kept repeating it to herself, maybe she'd train her subconscious that that was what Scott was, and someone she shouldn't go around kissing.

Even though she couldn't see him, Julianna could feel Scott's gaze on her.

"What?" She asked it like she hadn't just admitted that it had been him who had been keeping her up all night.

"Nothing. Just curious. What about me keeps you up at night, and why did it lead you here? You still wishing I had meant to shoot you? We can go down to the barn, and I can shoot you again on purpose, right here and now, if that would help you feel better."

Knowing that Scott couldn't see her, Julianna didn't bother to hide her smile. He was so cute sometimes. Or all the time, if she were being completely honest.

"No, I was being dumb about that whole thing. I was just thinking about how lucky I am to have a friend like you. I never thought that Scott Dallenforth would be as funny and—"

Her words were cut off by his lips on hers. They lingered, and the mint scent from his toothpaste washed over her.

"Please don't place me in the friend zone," he whispered, his breath tickling. "I've tried to respect your space, tried to give you what you need. I know that you want me to treat you like every other person at the ranch—like you don't mean more than a listening ear and someone to hang out with. But if giving you your space means I'm getting benched, I'd rather take the risk. Because I was serious about what I said earlier. I don't want to treat you like other people—like other girls. I'm falling for you, Jules."

There was something about the way he used her nickname in that moment—the nickname that only he used with her— that stripped Julianna of any hesitation. Yes, she might end up hurt by the end of the summer. But right here—right now—she couldn't say no to it. It would hurt worse than anything else she could possibly feel.

Like Scott had said, it was worth the risk.

So Julianna cupped a hand around the back of Scott's neck. It was dark enough that she missed, her lips landing on his jawline, and she swept them across as she felt for his mouth. A shudder from Scott told her that it may not have been a bad thing that she had missed. By the time her lips met his, Scott's arms were around her, holding her tight as if all the pent-up attraction and frustration exploded in a fiery moment of longing. Their lips danced as Julianna shifted her body so she'd be more comfortable, but in doing so, she managed to lose her balance and fall off the edge of the shed. She would have hit the dirt hard if Scott hadn't already been holding her so tightly.

Instead of letting go, he jumped off and fell to the dirt with her. It was a much softer landing than it would have been otherwise, and they lay together, tangled up in the dirt, half-laughing and trying to catch their breath.

"That was...interesting..." Scott said, his lips close to her ear. It tickled and sent a new wave of longing crashing through Julianna.

She passed her lips against his, and Scott's breath hitched when her flingers played with the hair at the back of his neck.

"I never knew someone could make me feel like this," he said when they finally came up for air.

Julianna smiled. "Feel like what?"

"Like I would lie in sagebrush every day if it meant that every time would be with you. Like I want to try my hardest to give you everything you've ever wanted. I want to make you laugh, see you smile. And kiss you. Definitely that one."

How was Julianna not going to kiss him again after something so sweet?

"I don't think I can stop," she whispered against his lips as her hands raked through his hair. "Seriously. I'm addicted."

"I'm more than happy to oblige," Scott said, his voice shaky.

Julianna laughed and pushed herself into him.

Except, this time it didn't lead to more kisses, but instead a shriek of pain from Scott. He leapt to his feet, inadvertently throwing Julianna in the process.

"Something just stung me. Or bit me. I can't tell." He sounded panicked, like it was more than just a little prick. Like it was something big.

Julianna leapt to her feet, not wanting the same treatment from whatever animals were out here. Not exactly the ending she had been hoping for this evening. "Let's get back to the barn."

"I don't know if I can."

Julianna heard the pain in his voice. Like this was much more than an ant bite. "We need to wake up Kat, have her check it out."

"Then they'll know we were out in the middle of the night."

Another groan of pain. "On second thought, I'll stay here while you go get her."

"And leave you alone with the wild animals? I don't think so. Where does it hurt?"

A pause. It left Julianna even more worried.

"My leg." It seemed Scott was having trouble talking, and when he tried to take a step, he stumbled.

"Hold up there, cowboy. Sling your arm around my shoulders."

And then Julianna half-dragged Scott Dallenforth to the RV where Kat lived. Thank goodness no one was around with their phones and cameras. She shuddered to think what the headlines on this one would read.

18

SCOTT

P ain. So much pain. Pounding. Whether it was in his head or it was Jules's fist on Kat's door, he wasn't sure.

Kat. In a T-shirt and pajama pants. He only noticed because they had Marvin the Martian on them. His favorite Loony Toons character. And one of the most underrated.

"Scott, I have to lift your pants leg," Kat said.

He wanted to protest. Wanted to tell her that it hurt too much, but he didn't have the energy. She tried to be careful—he could tell she was trying—but that didn't seem to make it any better. Scott cried out, the pain too much.

Kat's hands were soft. Gentle. Still too much pain.

"We have to take you to the ER," she said. Did this place even have a hospital?

Blueberries. What Scott wouldn't do for some blueberries at that moment. They reminded him of home. His mom put blueberries on everything.

Better yet, blueberry pancakes.

Would the hospital have blueberry pancakes?

Scott heard a man's voice. Sounded familiar. But then they lifted him, and it was too much.

Blackness.

Scott's eyes fluttered open. An empty room. Uncomfortable bed. Beeping.

"Oh, thank goodness."

Kat. She looked like she hadn't slept, her eyes puffy. Next to her was a sleeping pile of dirt. Jules. A couple branches of sagebrush still stuck out of her hair.

"We couldn't sleep," Scott murmured. "Went up to the paintball field. Didn't think to bring a headlamp." He felt himself drifting back to sleep. "That's my problem. I never think."

Kat stood and approached the bed. "Never mind that. You two aren't the first ones to wander around in the middle of the night at the ranch, and you won't be the last. I'm just grateful you're okay."

Scott's gaze found Jules again.

Kat smiled. "She stayed awake all night but finally gave in to exhaustion about fifteen minutes ago."

Scott noticed the sun was up, and probably had been for a while, judging by the amount of light in the room. His gaze returned to Kat.

"I don't remember much."

"You were stung by a scorpion. Did you know you're allergic?"

He shook his head, but it made his vision swim. Scott closed his eyes. "No. Never had the opportunity to find out."

He heard Kat chuckle. "Maybe stick to daytime wanderings for the time being." She paused. "I managed to keep this from the press, or at least for now. Once other people at the ranch catch wind of what happened, I'm not sure there's much I can do. With any luck, we can pass this off as you needing to leave to take care of some stuff for your upcoming tour, and they won't push it further. I've already spoken with your parents. They'll be on a flight that leaves in about an hour. You'll be going home with them."

Scott's eyes shot open. "What?"

"I don't blame them," Kat said, lifting one shoulder. "Apparently you're deathly allergic to the Arizona bark scorpion, and they don't want to take chances."

"We're in Utah, not Arizona."

Kat's lips twitched up. "I guess no one told the scorpions, because they haven't seemed to care much about state lines."

Scott released a long breath. "Do I get a say in this?"

This was where it was going to get complicated. He could tell by the way Kat hesitated. "You're eighteen. You signed the paperwork. Technically, yes, it is your decision."

"But...not technically?"

Kat played with a ring on her index finger, spinning it around. "Yours is an unusual situation. Keeping you here puts you at risk. There are a lot of people who have been calling me this morning—a lot of pressure from people who have an interest in you not dying."

"My manager," Scott said.

"And your parents."

The thought of leaving the ranch—leaving Jules—it felt like rocks had settled in his stomach. But at the same time, this had been what he'd wanted from the beginning. Not the getting stung by a scorpion and nearly dying part.

But this was it. Scott's way out.

He was going home.

SCOTT SNUGGLED UNDER HIS COVERS, the familiar scent of his mom's usual laundry detergent washing over him. It was good to be home. No bunk beds. No hiking up a hill just to take a shower. No prying off dirt-encased socks at the end of the day. No telling people not to swing guns in the direction of other people.

No scorpions.

His best friends were so excited to have him back that they were throwing him a party later that night. They had just returned from the trip that Scott was supposed to be on, but they said they wouldn't mind squeezing in another one before the end of the summer. Any excuse to get back to those beaches and waves and girls.

Scott was just the excuse they needed to get them there.

He smiled. This was how life was supposed to be. Impromptu trips. Parties. Unlimited food that didn't come from a cafeteria in a lodge.

His smile dipped, but he forced it back into place.

Scott had gotten really good at shoving down any feelings of regret that seemed to surface any time his thoughts remained on the ranch for too long—how things might have been if he hadn't been stung by that scorpion. Because when he let his thoughts wander back there, they inevitably landed on Jules. And that was one place he couldn't allow himself to go. It had been fun while it had lasted, but he'd known it was temporary. So had she.

He liked to think of that scorpion sting as a sign from the universe, or God, or whatever was out there. The ranch was not where Scott was meant to be.

Scott's parents didn't agree with this assessment. Even after his near-death experience, their stance on parties hadn't changed, and they weren't thrilled that he was jumping back into his former lifestyle so quickly. They had hoped at least a little bit of the ranch had rubbed off on him.

For a moment he'd thought it had. Thank goodness it hadn't

been a permanent change. Scott hadn't realized how close he'd been to losing his edge when he'd been in the thick of things. A sensitive country boy had no place on a stage. What was he going to do, become the ballad singer he'd been reduced to out there in Utah?

Not if he could help it. Tonight, he was going to make up for lost time and party like his career depended on it. Because, really, it did.

"THIS IS OFF THE HOOK," Scott yelled, attempting to be heard above the music. The bass was turned up so high that it was making ripples in the water of the swimming pool. His friends had spared no expense with the open bar and steady stream of scantily clad fans.

"It's not every day your bandmate and best friend comes back from the dead," Jordan yelled back. "No more running off to hicktown for you. It's bad for your health."

"I couldn't agree more."

At least, that was what he told everyone else—what he'd almost convinced himself of. But when Scott's phone exploded into song an hour later, and it came up as a Utah number, he held the phone in his hands, staring at the screen. Hesitating.

Memories of starlit nights washed over him. Jules's laugh and the way she looked holding a gun—like she was meant to take over the world. And the way she felt in his arms. It all came back—told him that had been the universe telling him where he was meant to be.

At the one place—with the one person—who had made him happy.

Jordan snatched the phone from Scott's hands and ended the call for him. Disappointment settled in Scott's stomach. It must have showed in his expression, because his friend raised an eyebrow, like he wanted an explanation of who had been on the other end of that phone call. Scott merely shot him a goofy grin. "The ranch wants me back. I was good publicity."

It hadn't been the first time someone had called from that number, and he always wondered if it was Jules. But he'd always ended up just staring—like that evening—until the phone had gone quiet, and the notification popped up that he'd missed a call.

Things were back to normal now. The way it should be. And there was no reason to mess all that up.

Right?

Jordan clapped him on the back and handed Scott his phone. "Way to stick it to the man. Now belly-flop from the top of the diving board and show everyone who the real Scott Dallenforth is." He started chanting, "Belly-flop. Belly-flop." It didn't take long for dozens of people to join in the chant.

Ouch. That sounded painful. Was that really who Scott Dallenforth was? Someone who would cause himself crazy amounts of pain just because everyone else wanted him to? Judging from the pictures that had ended up in the tabloids, yes, it was. Everyone wanted their rock stars a little on the crazy side, and Scott had delivered.

Scott hadn't felt the need to be that guy when he was on the ranch. No crazy stunts. It had been refreshing.

And now?

Scott tossed his phone onto the nearest pool chair as he stripped off his shirt. It burst into song again, vibrating, the same Utah number appearing on the screen, but it was drowned out by the cheers that exploded from the crowd as Scott climbed to the top of the diving board.

He still loved the sound of his name coming from a crowd,

loved the attention. But a twinge of guilt now accompanied it. An unease.

The chants pushed him forward, and he threw the crowd a grin.

And jumped.

19

JULIANNA

Julianna sent an elderly man down on the zipline, praying he wouldn't have a heart attack on the way. He hadn't seemed exactly confident as she'd sent him off the roof of the three-story barn.

Penny was up there with several of the kids from her camp, awaiting their turn. "You get ahold of Scott yet?" She pulled her newly dyed hair into a ponytail. It was red now, thanks to a prank gone wrong—or right, as it were.

A wave of bitter disappointment washed over Julianna. "No."

"I'm sure if something were wrong, we would have seen it in the news. People belly-flop from ridiculous heights all the time." Penny said it as if she were being helpful, but it only confirmed what Julianna had suspected. That Scott was fine, and he wanted nothing to do with her.

She had understood why he'd had to leave the ranch. The boy was deathly allergic to scorpions, and he may not be so lucky if he were on the receiving end of one of those stings again.

But Julianna had thought he'd changed—that he was more than how he appeared in the gossip magazines.

Except, more pictures had surfaced a few days earlier. Pictures of Scott that had been taken at a party, along with video of him purposely belly-flopping from a ridiculous height into a swimming pool. She had tried calling him that night—several times—and it had been the last time she'd tried.

Scott didn't need her anymore—not now that he had his old life back. He'd only needed her when she was the only option available.

"Yeah, I'm sure he's fine." Julianna tried to sound like she didn't care one way or the other.

"And he'll call."

Julianna stepped back so that Penny could move forward with the kids. "No. He won't." She rubbed a hand across her eyes. "He obviously saw this as a summer fling. I mean, the only reason I had his number was because I bribed Katie at the front desk to look in his file."

Penny smirked. "More like blackmailed."

That was true. Turned out Katie had been dating two guys from the ranch at the same time, and it was just Julianna's luck to catch her with the one that no one was supposed to know about. It was Scott's number for Julianna's silence. She was now wondering if that had been a mistake. Maybe it would have been better to leave things as "what might have been."

She looked out the window, across the trees, and into Zion National Park. It really was beautiful here. Maybe they kept on a few employees through the off-season, and she could postpone college and stay a little longer.

She released a long sigh. "He's moved on. And I should too."

Truthfully, she wasn't doing too badly. In the two weeks since Scott had left, Julianna had become better friends with the other girls in their little apartment, including Sandra. Turned out she was pretty cool when Julianna wasn't trying to break Sandra and Blair up.

Julianna and Penny were going out on a girls' movie night with their roomies after work, and it was the only thing getting Julianna through the last hour of zipline duty. They would have to drive an hour and a half to the nearest movie theater, so they'd get dinner on the way. And it couldn't come soon enough.

Penny was quiet as she helped the kids get their harnesses on, but then she glanced at Julianna. Her gaze had an excited glint to it—like she was up to something. "I think I might have something that will help you feel better."

"I'm not sure..." Julianna knew to be cautious whenever Penny got that glint in her eyes. Her friend had been involved in a feud with the boys at the ranch for the past couple of weeks, ever since they replaced her conditioner with hair dye.

"Please," Penny begged. "We'll be gone all night, so they won't be able to blame me for anything that might—or might not—happen. It will be perfect!"

Julianna released a hard breath but couldn't help smiling. "Fine. What did you have in mind?"

"Meet me upstairs in twenty minutes. The boys won't be off work yet, right?"

Julianna glanced at her watch. "No, they'll be cleaning up the equipment for at least another forty-five minutes."

"Perfect." And then Penny gave Julianna a grin that both made her nervous and helped her forget Scott. At least for the time being.

Penny had been right—a prank war was exactly what Julianna needed.

"I'M KEEPING WATCH—YOU do it," Julianna said. Butterflies filled her stomach, and she thought she might puke. This wasn't the type of thing she did—stealing things from the boys' dormitory.

What if they were caught? Could they be fired for doing this kind of thing?

"We'll have more chance of being caught if you don't help me, because it will take twice as long," Penny said, giving Julianna a little nudge toward the stairs that led to the boys' bunks.

Penny had a point, but Julianna still didn't like it.

She was not meant for a life of crime and had managed to keep herself out of Penny's shenanigans up until this point, which was pretty good, considering. Things had continued to escalate, though, and now here Julianna was. Stealing all the blankets and pillows off the boys' beds.

"Can we at least leave the pillows?" Julianna whispered as they climbed the stairs. "Most of them will have sleeping bags to use instead of blankets, but I'll feel bad if they have nothing but a hard bunk to lay their heads on. And then I'll break—the guilt will gnaw at me until I tell them it was us."

Penny laughed and shook her head. "All right. Just the blankets. That will help cut down the time and the space all this stuff will take up anyway."

Julianna had never moved so fast as she did when shoving those blankets into the large black garbage bags they had "borrowed" from the kids' camp. But when she approached an empty bunk against one of the far walls, she paused. Had this been Scott's bunk? It was in the furthest corner of the room and had a lonely feel about it.

She forced herself to walk away and not feel bad for the boy who obviously hadn't thought of her since he'd left. Scott was just fine—hadn't been traumatized by his brief foray into the real world. Her sympathy would only be wasted.

Once all the blankets were in the black bags, they stowed them in the closet where the kids' camp kept their supplies—a closet that only Penny and Sandra had the key for. And they'd both be gone for the evening.

Team Penny: 6

Team Boys: 5

As they drove through the canyon toward Cedar City, Julianna tried not to think about what would happen when the boys discovered their blankets missing. Sure, Penny would be gone for the evening, but Julianna knew the boys wouldn't be fooled. They'd know it was her. And there would be revenge.

THE REPERCUSSIONS WERE swift and strong. Taking those blankets had done more than require the boys to use their sleeping bags for an evening. It had apparently upended the entire ranch. The girls who had remained at the ranch had been even angrier than the guys—who, it turned out, hadn't been angry at all— letting the guys borrow some of their own supplies and expressing rage on their behalf.

And, of course, everyone knew who it had been. The next morning, Penny was on the receiving end of glares from every girl there, or at least those who hadn't been on the girls' trip. It was like a barrier of tension had been erected between the girls who slept in the barn versus the girls who slept under the lodge.

"I don't understand why the girls are mad," Penny whispered, sending anxious looks around her.

"Because most of them are dating at least one of the guys you pranked, and in some cases, more," Sandra said, her mouth full of eggs. She raised a shoulder. "Honestly, this was one of your tamer pranks. But definitely more creative than when you made those salty brownies. I mean, it was good, but kind of felt like you had run out of ideas, you know?"

Julianna laughed. Yeah, Sandra had definitely grown on her.

"I know what you mean," Penny said, chewing on a piece of

French toast stick. "But if this is how they react with something like this, I'm nervous about coming up with something bigger."

Blair walked up at that moment with a few other guys. They all wore smiles.

Uh-oh.

Blair slammed his hands down on the end of the table, though his smile hadn't diminished. "You know we're not going to let this one go, right?"

Penny returned his smile. "As opposed to all the other pranks I've pulled? I mean, really, taking your and your friends' clothes from the laundry and hanging them to dry on the zipline was one of my personal favorites. Did Sandra know you have hearts on your socks?"

Blair's eyes flashed, but his smile managed to stay intact. "She gave them to me."

Julianna glanced at Sandra and noticed her cheeks had gone red.

"We were going through the awkward phase where you give an anniversary gift every month. We were celebrating two months," she murmured, while also sinking in her seat.

Penny must have known she had gotten under Blair's skin, because her grin grew wider. She leaned back in her chair, folding her arms across her chest. "Mazel tov. But in all serious-ness, what is it about your blankets that has the ranch up in arms? I truly don't understand."

"Never mind the why," Cameron said, stepping up from behind his friend. "It's the *how* that you should be worried about. As in, how are we going to repay you?"

Blair shot Cameron a warning glance, like he'd already said too much.

And that one look made Julianna more nervous than anything else.

THERE WAS nothing like a day off work and spending it all in the pool. Eventually, though, Julianna's fingers wrinkled to the point her hands could be featured in a senior citizen commercial.

"I think I'm done," Julianna said, pulling herself from the water.

Penny followed suit and wrung her hair out. "I'm right behind you."

Julianna wrapped her towel around her waist and twisted her hair into a bun. "After spending the past three hours in the pool, I'm looking forward to a nice hot shower and then collapsing in front of the TV in the lounge."

The pool was right next to the lodge, so she had walked over barefoot, something Julianna now regretted as the sidewalk was a lot hotter than it had been three hours earlier. "Ouch, ouch, ouch." She looked like she was doing an Irish jig as she jumped her way to the stairwell that led down to their apartment.

Penny laughed. "I warned you."

"You sound like my mom." As soon as they were in the apartment, Julianna dropped her towel and smooshed it into a ball. "Think I can make it into my laundry hamper from here?"

Penny squinted and tapped her chin, like she was trying to judge the distance. "You'll have to make it clear across the bathroom, and it will have to still be high enough to drop in. If we were making a bet, I'd say no."

"Then let's make it a bet." Julianna grinned. "If I make it in, you have to finally kiss Andy. I still can't believe you two haven't done it already."

Penny's cheeks pinked. "We're taking it slow."

"That would be great, if this wasn't a summer fling. But we only have four weeks left here, and time is something that is not on your side."

Penny lifted a shoulder. "Maybe I don't see this as a summer fling."

Julianna stared. Wow, her friend really liked the guy. It made her heart heavy. Hadn't she seen Scott as more than a summer fling—hoped it was more—even though it was destined to end? It was only going to make things harder for Penny when it was time to leave. When it was time for them to go their separate ways, live their separate lives.

But Julianna wasn't going to be the one to rain on her friend's parade—she was tired of being the realist, the one who didn't take chances. Maybe if Julianna had taken more chances, Scott would still be at the ranch. Or at least answering her calls.

She shot her friend a smile. "I'm happy for you."

Relief passed over Penny's features. "Thanks. Me too." She threw her shoulders back. "Now for that hot shower."

"No...now for my epic towel shot across the bathroom. *Then* the hot shower."

As Julianna cocked her arm back, though knowing this was an impossible shot, Penny jumped in front of her.

"Wait. We never decided what you have to do if you don't make it."

Right. Bets were usually two-sided. But it was a lot more fun when Julianna didn't have anything at stake.

"Nah, it's all right. This will just be for fun."

Penny grinned. "No way. If you don't make this shot, you have to finally leave a message on Scott's phone." When Julianna opened her mouth to protest, Penny shook her head. "I know you always hang up just before the beep."

Julianna didn't like this turn of events. It was one thing to challenge her friend to kiss someone she already knew liked her. It was another thing for Julianna to contact Scott, who had obviously already moved on and didn't want to hear from her. She could handle him not answering her calls, but she didn't know if she'd be able to handle him not returning them.

But Penny was giving her a look that said she wasn't going to take no for an answer, her arms crossed across her chest and her eyebrow raised—challenging her.

"Fine," Julianna said, releasing a long breath. And then, under that same breath, she muttered, "I better make this shot."

She motioned for Penny to move aside, then once again cocked her arm back, the towel ball on the verge of falling apart. Crap. This thing was not very stable.

Julianna let her arm fly...and the towel landed with a thud four feet in front of her.

"That was a practice shot," she yelled, running forward and grabbing the towel and throwing it again. It went another three feet, landing in the center of the bathroom. "One more try," she yelled over her shoulder, panic lacing her words. She could *not* call Scott again. And she was definitely not going to leave a message for him. A message that told him how desperate she was—how she wasn't over him. Just like every other girl.

And that was the problem, wasn't it? She'd become what she'd been terrified of from the very beginning.

Julianna had become like every other girl—and Scott knew it. And now he didn't want her—didn't need her.

She ran to grab the towel, but as she snatched it up, she realized there was something under the towel. Something long and scaled.

"Rattlesnake!"

Julianna jumped onto the counter as Penny screamed from the other side of the room.

"Are you kidding me?" Penny yelled before bolting out the door. Julianna hoped it was to get help and that her friend hadn't just abandoned her, leaving her to figure out the snake situation on her own.

Julianna eyed the snake, then scooted along the counter's edge, her feet tucked up under her. There was something strange about the snake, though. Julianna's heart calmed enough for her to realize that it wasn't moving. And its head was tucked under another towel. Almost like...

"Aww," she groaned. "This isn't even my fight!" Julianna dropped from the counter, then noticed the video camera set up in the laundry room that was pointed her way.

She snatched up the second towel and saw that it was indeed a real snake, but the head had been cut off.

Before Julianna had the chance to register whether she was grossed out, impressed, or just mad, the apartment door burst open. She spun around, expecting to see Jimmy, or maybe Kat, but was instead met by someone who shouldn't even be at the ranch.

"Scott!"

She was more stunned to see him standing there, shovel in hand, than she had been to see the rattlesnake. So she stared. And didn't say anything. How could she when her emotions were tangled together, each fighting for dominance.

Part of her wanted to run to him and wrap her arms around his neck and give him a kiss that would ensure he'd never want to leave again. The other part wanted to still run to him, but rather than wrap him in her arms, it would be her hands that would be doing the wrangling as she wrung his neck.

How dare he just show up like this, like everything was fine and he hadn't been gone for three weeks, never answering her calls?

But Scott didn't seem interested in Julianna at the moment, his gaze bouncing around the room wildly. "Where is it?"

She folded her arms over her chest and gave him the best glare she knew how. "Where's what?"

Scott gave the shovel an impatient shake in Julianna's direction. "The snake. Penny said there's a rattlesnake in your place."

Julianna sounded almost bored as she gave a nod toward the bathroom. "In there. But it's already dead."

He slowly lowered the shovel until it hung at his side. "You... killed the snake?"

"Would have, if it hadn't already been dead." As if Julianna had been just about to take care of the snake herself, like it was no big deal. And like she wasn't terrified of anything that moved. When Scott raised an eyebrow, knowing there was no way Julianna would have killed that thing herself, she said, "It was a prank by the boys. To get back at Penny. She started a bit of a prank war shortly after you left. Looks like the ball is in our court, but it will be tough to beat something like this."

Scott looked from Julianna to the shovel, then back to Julianna. "Looks like you have everything under control, so I guess I'll—"

"What are you doing here?" Julianna took a step toward Scott, no longer nervous around the rock star. Because that wasn't who he was to her—not anymore. He'd transformed into a regular guy while at the ranch—one who was as kind as he was good-looking. Not to mention being Julianna's first kiss. He had also been one of the best friends she'd ever had.

Until he'd left.

"I-I work here," he said, seeming taken aback by the force behind Julianna's words.

"No. You don't. You used to work here. Before you went home. Before you went back to being Scott Dallenforth, party king. Before you didn't take my calls." Julianna's voice broke on the last word, betraying the emotions she had been working so hard to keep buried.

In a vain attempt to maintain her dignity—or at least not feel like a complete loser, melting down in front of Scott, who had

had his arms around a different girl every night since leaving—
Julianna turned and stomped into the bathroom. She didn't look
back as she wrapped the snake in one of the towels and then
returned and shoved it into Scott's arms.

He nearly dropped the shovel as he attempted to keep the
snake from falling to the floor, but his gaze never left Julianna
through it all. It was curious and searching—and even seemed
hurt.

"I didn't ignore your phone calls," Scott said, his voice quiet.
"I never got them."

"That's funny, because it was your voice on the voicemail
greeting."

Scott remained quiet, his head tilting to the side. "You left a
message?"

Heat rushed into Julianna's cheeks. "Well, no. But I called
like fifteen times." Realizing how desperate and stalkerish that
sounded, she said, "Or at least it felt like it. Might have been just
two or three. I wasn't keeping track."

She squeezed her hands into fists, frustrated that she'd gone
from being in charge of the conversation—strong and confident
—to ending up where she always did. At the bottom, begging for
the guy to like her.

"It doesn't matter much," Julianna said, steeling herself for
whatever charm Scott might send her way. "Deliver that snake to
Blair and Cameron, though, won't you? Preferably under their
bedsheets." She then pushed Scott out the door, shutting it
behind him before he had the chance to protest.

She leaned against the door, breathing heavily. Of all the
scenarios she'd played out in her head if she ever had the
chance to see Scott again—this had not been one of them.

20

SCOTT

Scott stood outside the girls' apartment. He knew he couldn't go back in, but he also didn't want to leave.

That Utah number that had called repeatedly. He'd known it had been the ranch. Sure, he'd said it was probably them just wanting their PR guy back. But he'd wondered if it was Jules—hoped it was. She would have had to use the ranch's landline, since there was no cell service.

And that had been the real reason he hadn't answered. Not because he didn't want to talk to her—he did. Desperately. But he'd thought she'd convince him to leave everything and come back to the ranch—because he would have.

And that scared him. That something, or someone, could ever convince him to walk away from everything he had in California. For a summer fling, and a ranch where he slept in a barn with twenty other guys.

That wasn't the life for him.

Or so he'd thought.

"Hey, looks like you took good care of that snake," Penny said, startling Scott out of his thoughts. She walked down the steps toward the apartment, though her voice wavered and she skirted around him, like she didn't want to get too close.

"Nah, Jules had it under control," he said. "I'm just the garbage guy, taking it out to the trash."

"Julianna did that?" Penny asked, raising both eyebrows. "I'm impressed."

"Yeah, well, people tend to underestimate her. Take her for granted."

The way he said it—Penny must have known he wasn't talking about the snake. Her expression softened, and she leaned against the wall. "Look, I like you, Scott. But Julianna had a rough time of it after you left. I mean, she understood why you couldn't come back, but then it was like—" She paused, like she was trying to find the right words. "The problem with dating a celebrity is that you know what they're doing when they're not with you. Julianna saw the pictures of you at the parties, with the other girls—she knew who you were with when you weren't answering her calls. And then the past week she finally started doing better. Even got in on the prank war and going out for girls' nights and everything. It's...not good that you've just shown up like this."

Scott knew that. He knew it wasn't fair of him. But going home—it had been what he'd needed to realize where he needed to be, and who he needed to be with. And it wasn't California.

He gave a curt nod and trudged up the stairs, attempting to keep the snake from slipping out from the towel. It was giving him the heebie jeebies, and Scott couldn't be rid of it fast enough. He paused on the top step, however, and shot a glance over his shoulder. "Will you at least ask Jules to meet me at the paintball field? Tell her I'll be there at nine o'clock, whether she decides to show up or not."

Penny seemed uncomfortable as she squirmed where she stood at the bottom of the stairs. "I don't know, Scott..."

"I'm going to be there one way or another, so you might as well pass on the message." And then he left to dispose of the rattlesnake.

Handling a dead snake was one thing that hadn't made it onto his bucket list, and something he hoped to never have to do again.

SCOTT STRUMMED his guitar as he sat on the edge of the paintball shed. He'd missed it while away—funny the things that take on nostalgic value when you think you'll never see it again.

He played a few riffs, then began playing a song he'd been working on. Scott was a bundle of nerves, and playing helped calm him. He'd been doing a lot of original songs in the past couple of weeks—songs that his recording studio would never approve of.

When he was halfway through the second verse, he heard the crunching of rocks. He kept playing.

The sun was sinking but not yet completely gone, and in its fading light, he watched as Jules climbed the last of the hill. She walked over and jumped up next to him on the ledge of the shed, though averting her gaze all the while.

When Scott continued playing, she said, "You ask me out here for a private concert?"

His fingers paused, the sound gradually fading. "You were right. I was avoiding your calls. I mean I wasn't sure it was you, but I thought it might have been."

Jules's gaze whipped toward him, and then she slowly shook her head. "Well, at least you get to the point." She then jumped from the shed and looked like she was ready to take off at a run.

Scott laid his guitar down and jumped out after her, laying a hand on her arm. "You don't understand. I also returned because of you."

She stilled but didn't turn back. "Then you're lousy at avoiding people you don't want to talk to."

Scott chuckled, even as his heart tied itself into knots. "Good thing, too." His hands were sweaty, but he was too afraid to remove his hand from Jules's arm. If he did, he might lose her for good. "Otherwise, I might have made the biggest mistake of my life."

That made Jules turn, but only slightly. "Meaning?"

"Meaning that the life you've been watching me lead—the one in California—it's ridiculous. A show. Something to get me into papers. And it's not worth it. Not anymore."

Jules fully turned now, an eyebrow raised in skepticism. "What are you saying? That you're giving up your career?" Her voice held doubt—and disappointment. Never mind that that wasn't at all what Scott had intended. Was she only interested in dating him if he was a rock star?

Seeming to sense his confusion, she quickly said, "It's fine if you are. I just... You love music."

Scott smiled and moved in close, hoping it wouldn't scare Jules away. "Yes, I do love music. And I'm not giving up my career. I'm just...taking it in a new direction. And it's all because of you. And this crazy ranch."

Jules hesitated, like she was still unsure what his intentions were—his motivation. If he could be trusted.

"Look," Scott said, deciding he needed to use a different tactic—a more visual one. He lifted his shirt.

At first Jules took a step back and averted her eyes, but curiosity got the best of her, and she glanced at him. All hesitation disappeared, and her eyes widened. "What happened?"

She stepped forward and reached out toward the black and

blue bruises that were beginning to yellow. They covered his chest and torso.

"I was dared to do a belly-flop off the diving board. Didn't want to, knew it was going to hurt like hell. But it's hard to say no to something when everyone's chanting your name."

Jules seemed transfixed by the bruises, not wanting to touch them but unable to look away. "I saw the video."

"Everyone did. Went viral, as I'm sure my publicist hoped it would." He paused and lowered his shirt. "Which solidified in everyone's mind that I'm nothing more than a brainless singer who will do anything anyone asks of him. They think of me as an idiot who only knows how to play the guitar and get plastered."

"If it's any consolation, that's how people see most rock stars."

That only further solidified Scott's resolve to change his image. "I don't want to be that person. I don't want to do belly-flops because I'm afraid to say no. I don't want to wake up to a hangover every morning. I'm tired of being spineless."

He sucked in a shuddered breath and reached for Jules's hand, desperately hoping she wouldn't pull away. She didn't. Scott wrapped his fingers around hers.

"It was when I hit the water, pain shooting through my body, wondering if I had broken all my bones, that I knew I couldn't go back to who I've been for the past three years. The ranch changed me—you changed me. You saw me for who I could be without all the expectations. And when I hit that water—it scared me. I knew I had to get back here. Scorpions included. And apparently rattlesnakes."

Jules's lips twitched up at the corners, and she ran her free hand through her hair. "You ran in to save me from that rattlesnake."

"Yes, I did. And trust me when I say that Blair isn't going to love the surprise that's awaiting him when he goes to bed tonight."

She released a shocked laugh. "You actually did that?"

"You asked me to."

Jules hadn't been serious about that? He really was a pushover who would do anything. But when it came to Jules, he didn't mind so much.

"I know, but...well, I didn't think you'd actually do it." She paused, her lips pulling down. "I appreciate the effort, Scott. I really do."

Scott sensed there was a "but" in there somewhere. He raised an eyebrow, encouraging her to continue.

"But, as nice as it is to see you, I don't want you back here if you're just going to leave again. If you're going to get bored or realize that returning was career suicide. Or that you prefer California girls. I told you that you can't treat me like the others, coming and going as you please. I meant it."

Scott tightened his fingers around Jules's. "I know. And even though going home wasn't my idea, I didn't fight it either. I let you down. And I don't blame you for being mad. You should be." His gaze met hers. "All I can ask for is your forgiveness."

He didn't expect his words to have any effect—too little, too late, and all that. But then Jules pulled him in and laid a long kiss on his lips.

When they pulled apart, he tucked a lock of Jules's hair behind her ear and gave her a crooked smile. "What was that for?"

"For coming back."

His gaze fell to the ground. "I'm sorry I avoided your calls. Part of it was guilt. And the other was that I was afraid you'd try to get me to come back—to give up the type of life I was used to. And I was afraid that I liked you so much, I just might do it."

She tilted her head to the side. "Which you did anyway."

"Yup. Shows what kind of power you have over me."

Jules pulled him in like she was going for another kiss, but then whispered against his lips, "I approve of you shedding your bad boy rock-star image, but please don't give your music up. I don't want to be one of those girls who breaks up the band."

Scott laughed, then let his lips land on hers. "Never." When he pulled away, he said, "I go on tour next month. Want to come with?"

Jules hesitated. Not the reaction he'd been hoping for. "Go on tour with Scott Dallenforth—every girl's dream."

Why didn't she sound excited about the prospect? Was it wrong that he'd asked? It had seemed right in the moment, but it was probably too soon. He's just gotten her to forgive him, after all.

"You don't have to. Just thinking out loud," he said quickly. "If you're bored and looking for something to do, the option is open."

"I'm supposed to start college in the fall," she said slowly. "But I suppose I could take classes online."

He didn't dare to hope, but when she didn't continue, he tentatively asked, "So...does that mean you'll come?"

Jules's gaze met his, and she burst into a grin. "Are you kidding? Of course I'll come." She paused, and her smile dipped. "But only because I'm going to be mind-numbingly bored at school all semester. I mean, why else would a girl agree to go on tour with one of the hottest singers in America?"

Her grin returned, and Scott couldn't help but match it. He didn't know what to expect, didn't know if this—whatever it was —would last beyond the fall. Maybe she'd realize that dating a rock star wasn't all it was cracked up to be. Maybe she'd find being on a tour bus all day and in hotels every night annoying— maybe she'd find *him* annoying.

But then Jules pulled out her phone. After a couple of quick swipes, his band's latest song began playing. It was a love song, and sappy. Not Scott's favorite. She held out a hand to him, like she wanted him to join her.

"Dance with me?"

Scott took her hand. "All right, but only if we change the song. I really don't love that one, and I'm going to have to sing it hundreds of times once we go on tour."

Jules cocked her head to the side and smiled. "All right. You have something better in mind?"

He pulled his own phone from his pocket, his finger hesitating over the screen before pressing play. Slow notes filled the air—the same notes he'd played the night they'd all camped outside—the night he'd shared Jules's pillow. He set the phone down on the paintball shed.

"I thought you said this song hadn't been recorded—that it was an impromptu thing," Jules said.

Scott placed his other hand on the small of her back, and they began to sway to the music. It felt good—right—holding her in his arms.

He shuddered to think it was something he'd almost given up.

"It was," he said, his voice low next to her ear. He felt her shiver, and he pulled her in tighter. "I thought about what you'd said about how I should do more stuff like it, and I decided to record it in my buddy's studio. He loved it. Said this was what I should have been doing all along. Figured I'd record a few songs before presenting it to my producer." He raised a shoulder. "Don't think they'll go for it, but I figure it's worth a shot."

"So you'd...what...go solo?"

"No," he said quickly, not wanting to entertain the possibility. Not wanting to think about what that would do to Matt and Jordan. But wasn't that what he was suggesting? "At least, not if I can get the rest of the band on board with it. I'm just tired of having no say in the creative process, you know? Tired of being synthetic."

Jules laid her head on his shoulder. "Well, whatever you decide, know that I'll be right there by your side, keeping it real. I mean, someone has to remind you where you come from, cowboy."

"And I wouldn't want it to be anyone but you."

EPILOGUE

One year later

Julianna buried her head into Scott's arm. "This is so embarrassing." They were sitting on the couch in the top of the barn, and they were surrounded by half the people who had worked at the ranch the previous year. The big-screen TV in front of them began playing the home video that Blair and Cameron had taken of the girls when they'd discovered the rattlesnake.

"You realize how wrong this is, right?" Penny said, throwing a scowl at Blair. "What if we had been changing clothes?"

Cameron threw his arm around Amanda's shoulders and gave her a little squeeze. "Relax. I asked Amanda to make sure that didn't happen. And we wouldn't be here watching it if anything risqué happened. This video is rated PG."

"Amanda wasn't even there," Julianna said, lifting her head.

Amanda threw them an apologetic smile. "You guys were in the pool forever. I got tired of waiting."

"Why are we even watching this? This was so last year," Penny groaned.

"Because you're adorable in it," Andy said. "Look at me, dating a movie star." And then he sneaked in a kiss that was so quick, Julianna almost missed it. Those two were seriously adorable and had the whole long-distance dating thing down, but because they'd spent most of it apart, they hadn't figured out the whole public-displays-of-affection thing. Even holding hands in public embarrassed them.

In the video, Scott entered the apartment, and Julianna realized what was about to happen. This was when Scott had returned from California—when Julianna had still been angry with him. They'd been completely awkward, and then she'd thrown the rattlesnake at Scott, instructing him to put it in Blair's bed.

She leaped up from the couch. "Well, I think we got all our reactions. Sandra apparently cursed it with every type of voodoo magic she knows before running out of the apartment prior to our arrival, and we all saw Penny's brave exit." Julianna grabbed the remote out of Blair's hand and turned off the TV.

"Hey, we were watching that," Cameron protested.

"The rest of it is boring. Besides, don't we have newbies to train?" She tossed a smile at Scott. "And by newbies, I mean you. You've been on the road so long, I may have to retrain you how to use that lasso of yours."

Scott laughed. "One, you were on the road with me, so you have no room to talk. And two, I can still out-lasso you any day of the week."

It wasn't hard when neither of them had ever figured out what the heck to do with a rope. But they had figured out what to do in the back of a tour bus, stealing kisses when everyone else was asleep. And when they were awake. The past year had changed Julianna's life for the better—and Scott's.

He'd somehow managed to completely transform his image (Julianna had helped with that, given that Scott was now a one-woman kind of man) and his sound, and everyone was going nuts for it. Even his bandmates, who had been a bit skeptical at first, had to admit that they loved the changes. They weren't the only ones. Scott's band was more famous now, and more liked, than when Scott had been trying so hard to make everyone happy.

The best part? He'd hired Julianna as an assistant tour manager, which meant that for the time being, she was doing school virtually, and she never had to say good-bye. Everyone else had thought they'd be sick of each other by now. But if anything, the opposite was true.

Julianna smiled and jumped back onto the couch next to Scott.

"You're trying to change the subject," Blair said, and grabbed the remote back from her. "Don't forget, I've seen the whole video. And yes, I know the rattlesnake in my bed was your doing."

Sandra nodded. "True. But I don't think the whole ranch needs to see it. You already got to show our completely fake reactions to your obviously dead rattlesnake. That should be enough."

"You did not know it was dead," Blair said with a laugh. "But I'll go with it, mostly because Jules is right. We have our first staff meeting of the summer to get to."

"Since when does anyone but me call you Jules?" Scott whispered.

Julianna didn't know when things had changed, but sometime in the last year, she'd become less Julianna and more Jules. And people had noticed.

She gave him a teasing smile. "I kind of like it. Like you said when we first met, it suits me."

"But what am I going to call you now?" Scott asked with mock frustration. "I can't call you the same thing everyone else is."

Jules kissed his pursed lips. "You have the rest of forever to figure it out."

ALSO BY KAT BELLEMORE

ABOUT THE AUTHOR

Kat Bellemore is the author of the Borrowing Amor sweet romance series. Deciding to have New Mexico as the setting for the series was an easy choice, considering its amazing sunsets, blue skies and tasty green chile. That, and she currently lives there with her husband and two cute kids. They hope to one day add a dog to the family, but for now, the native animals of the desert will have to do. Though, Kat wouldn't mind ridding the world of scorpions and centipedes. They're just mean.
You can visit Kat at www.kat-bellemore.com.